"A very funny account of cryptozoological shenanigans on the edge of urban Banstead. It's not often these days that I laugh out loud when reading a book, but this one is rich with brilliant comic moments. Loved it."
Gareth E. Rees, author of *Unofficial Britain* and *Car Park Life*

"This tale of what happens when a hobby becomes an obsession is unlike anything I've read before. Absurd and inventive, *Gigantic* made me laugh and shake my head in equal measure, and the ingenious way in which the story unfolds had me gripped."
Lucie McKnight Hardy, author of *Water Shall Refuse Them*

Also available from Unsung Stories

GIGANTIC

ASHLEY STOKES

UNSUNG
STORIES

Published by Unsung Stories

3 Rosslyn Road
London E17 9EU, United Kingdom

www.unsungstories.co.uk

First edition published in 2021
First impression

Paperback ISBN: 978-1-912658-14-5
ePub ISBN: 978-1-912658-15-2

Edited by Dan Coxon
Proofreading by Jonathan Oliver

Cover Artwork © Nicolas Ruston 2021

Cover design by Vince Haig
Text design by Cox Design Limited
Typesetting by Vince Haig

Printed in the UK by Clays Ltd, Elcograf S.p.A.

Dedicated to the Memory of the 1970s

Dear Mate,

I wasn't sure you would get this far, so thanks a million already. You opened the mystery bag. Many wouldn't have had the conkers to open the mystery bag. The world is made up of two types of people: those who creep through life, terrified of the mystery bag; and those who ride to the edge of human knowledge just to get a peek of what's inside the mystery bag.

I'm one of the riders now. Kevin Stubbs is one of those guys.

Inside the bag, along with this letter, is a dossier that describes the whole story. I expect you've already heard about it, given it all kicked off in our home town.

I notice you don't live there anymore. You escaped to somewhere nice and safe where the great mysteries do not peep at you from behind the trees in the dead of night. If you had stayed, you could have been in on it from the start, the Great Confirmation.

You used to be into this stuff, remember? I remember. Of course I remember. It's still all lit up for me. Always will be.

You must recall that my mum was very religious, a proper Jehovah's Witness. I wasn't allowed to read or see anything that wasn't basically *The Watchtower*. I especially wasn't allowed exposure to any of what she called 'inappropriate' or 'fanciful', or 'demonic' – anything good, basically, that I liked. I can tell you now, because I'm not ashamed of it anymore, but my earliest memory of her is being in a shop and throwing a proper wobbler because she wouldn't buy me the Ladybird *Dracula*. 'It's not appropriate,' she kept saying, over and over until she was shouting and we were asked to leave. I just about got away with reading those terrifying C.S. Lewis Narnia books because she read somewhere they were Christian really. She's passed on now, so I can do what I like.

But when we were kids, you were the lifesaver. Without being friends with you at school and being allowed round your house sometimes, I wouldn't have known anything. I would have stayed ignorant. We used to go to the library together and get out all the books about weird goings-on, remember? You used to hide my stash of magazines like *Omni* and *The Unexplained*, anything that had articles about mysterious creatures, especially the

yeti or the 1967 Patterson–Gimlin Bigfoot
sighting at Bluff Creek, California. That
was always the big one, the film that
started it all.

We first saw it round your house, on
Arthur C. Clarke's Mysterious World.
There it was: gigantic, hairy, with long,
swinging arms and a cone-shaped cranium.
I was on fire. I was amazed. The world
wasn't like it was explained in the Bible
and *The Watchtower*. Monsters were real,
and not only were they real, they were
good.

We went over all this like proper
investigators, remember? Talked about how
we wished this stuff happened where we
lived, south of the river, north of the
hills, and not always abroad in foreign
countries. That's when it started for me.

I wanted to see things.

You wanted to see things, once.

Then: you remember, yonks ago, you
must have come back on a break from your
studies, and you and me, old mates, we
bump into each other in the Butterchurn
pub, aka The Churn. And I come over,
hadn't seen you since school, and we get
chatting. And I told you. I told you it
was HERE. It was not just in America and
the Himalayas; it was HERE, in SUTTON. I
had seen it on TV. I had tracked down the

men who filmed it. I had joined up, gone
looking for it with them. I had seen it
myself, TWICE, once in the cemetery and
once outside the hospital, FACT.

And what did you do? You said you were
getting me a drink. Did you get me a
drink? No. You legged it.

All is forgiven, though. I'm putting all
my trust in you by letting you in on
what we call the Great Confirmation. What
you've got here in this dossier is the
truth and the lies, the official and the
unofficial versions, the cover-up and the
true story. You get her side of things,
Maxine Cash's official report, and then
I comment on her theories with what I
believe is the true, factual story.

If you don't hear from me in three months'
time, you'll want to make three copies of
this document. Post one to the *Daily Mail*
and one to Oliver Koch at the Department
of Fortean Zoology in Exeter. Hold on to
the third copy.

This is the important bit.

I don't trust the postal service where
I am now, so I've put a letter to my boy
inside the mystery bag as well. I want
you to stick a postage stamp on it and put
it in a post box so he gets it tomorrow.

You will hear from me again, but if
you don't and three years go by, send

the third copy of the dossier to my boy. He'll be old enough then.

As I say, there is no one else I can trust. And, remember, as you read through it: this is not a hoax, FACT.

Best wishes

Kevin Stubbs

GIGANTOPITHECUS INTELLIGENCE TEAM

REPORT #214 (CATEGORY A)

SECTION 1

Submitted by Witness: Monday, 8 July ███████

SUMMARY: A man filming a children's party on common land reports sighting a large ape-like biped moving through nearby trees

---

NEAREST TOWN: Sutton, Surrey

REPORT #214:
THE FACTS BY KEVIN STUBBS:
SECTION ONE

The first throb of Report #214 buzzed against my thigh at the same time as my internal sonar picked up two sets of footfalls heading towards my workstation. You can't spend 10,000 hours out in the woods, kitted up and shoulder-to-shoulder with your team, without developing super-surveillance hearing skills. These can prove as useful in the office as they do out in the Great Spaces.

One set belonged to Clive. I recognised his slightly uneven way of walking. Before he joined iiSkipper, he used to be a recruitment widget for Homebase. During a team-bonding weekend in Chislehurst he'd crashed a quad bike into a hospitality tent and spannered his knee.

I shouldn't know this.

He doesn't know that I know this.

Clive is Head of HR at iiSkipper, which is (not down to him) the highest ranking UK reverse auction skip hire site on Google. I was its IT Support.

He had a woman with him. I hunched over my workstation and pretended to concentrate on isolating the plug-in that was causing a load of stress and grief to our registrations database. Clive was introducing the woman to all the other iiSkipper pod droids. Soon they would trespass on my domain. After they left I would check the text message that had just buzzed against my thigh.

It was 3.15 in the afternoon.

Outside, it was Sutton.

I did not yet know that I had been waiting for this moment for all my life.

I wasn't too fussed about the text message at first. I expected it was from Bohuslava (aka my wife). Or separated wife, estranged wife. I don't know. We were not divorced yet. It was all undecided, up in the air. That's how I liked to think about it. A few days before I had put out some feelers about seeing our boy again, now that so much time had passed since the business with the van. I was pretty sure this text was her telling me again that he still didn't want to come out and see a film with me, go for a burger, or bowling or go-karting or for an unforgettable adventure in the woods, or see me ever again, ever, unless I changed. I didn't want to be reminded of this while Clive was around and I ought to be on my best behaviour.

Anyway, Clive appeared outside my workstation and introduced me to this blonde he called Becca, our new 'Fulfillment Executive' (aka someone with no more job satisfaction than Walter the Wobot, that stainless-steel butler with the coffee machine for a stomach and a TV for a head that used to be in *Judge Dredd*). This Becca would be working very closely with Clive, which I'm sure was not what she imagined she'd be getting for her thirty-grand's worth of student fees and three years writing essays on Oasis lyrics, or whatever they do at those places. I'm not like her. I'm not like him. I live for the night-time. I live for the woods. The Great Spaces, the Great Outdoors. I work only to live, and I live to Know.

'This is Kevin,' said Clive. 'Your first stop if your email doesn't work.'

'Welcome to the Jungle,' I said.

'Hiya.' She looked away, quick-sharp.

'C'mon, Becca,' said Clive. 'Let's introduce you to the marketing team. They're a great team. You'll soon find at ii, it's all about the team.'

Teams. What did he really know about teams?

I rolled my chair backwards and made sure they were gone. None of the others registered me. They stayed in their pods. Back in my pod, I stared at the teak-effect partitions that I liked to keep nice and blank, to help keep me nice and blank and focused. My phone buzzed in my pocket again. What did she want now?

The message was not from Boho, but from my valued colleague and fellow investigator into night-time mysteries, Derek Funnel (aka The Funnel).

The Long Man Cometh.

I looked around for anyone else watching me in the pod droid hangar, kept myself together, and then checked my personal email on my phone. There it was: the message alert from our website.

Report #214 had finally arrived.

> • <

The significance of Report #214 was immediately obvious to me. The North Surrey Gigantopithecus had been seen again, but this time not by a headcase or some spliffed-up kids or a posse of drunks after the pubs chucked out, but by a large group of respectable people.

More importantly, they had film.

We hadn't had footage since the Gartree-Hogg film that

started it all. There was only one other film, but none of us had seen that, it was that hushed up by the government. It also looked like The Funnel and I had managed to see the report before our Lead Investigator, Maxine Cash (aka Sci-Borg), could dismiss it right off the bat.

She's a school teacher, a science teacher at that, and her big idea was that we needed to use scientific methods when we investigated the greatest mystery in human evolution that we were lucky to have on our doorstep, when usually these things only happen in places like California, Canada or Nepal – abroad, basically. She said we'd been 'slipshod' in the past and we needed to be more rigorous and more sceptical, like her. I saw the sense in this, and I tried to go along with it and learn from her, but it didn't matter in the end because it was real. I'd seen it loads of times. All we needed was footage. Even she couldn't dismiss footage.

So there's me, stuck at work when all I wanted to do was sling on the kit and bomb round the witness's house right that second.

My phone vibrated again.

It was The Funnel: *Sci-Borg has deployed the dampening field.*

I checked the GIT WhatsApp group.

RE Report #214: I know you boys are probably overexcited already, but we can't at this stage rule out the possibility that this is yet another clear case of misidentification. I will contact the witness this afternoon and report back to you if I feel that our time is best spent investigating this one further.

She'd basically dropped off the landing craft and was stumbling up the beach with the *preconception* that this was just another case of someone not knowing how to focus their camera, or not realising that if you film a dog standing on its hind legs, or even some people from a certain distance, the image will blur and look a bit like a Bigfoot. This is really why I should have been Lead Investigator. She'd only been with us for about a year. For now, though, I was happy to do as I'd been told by her predecessor, bide my time, and try it her way until we finally nailed it.

I left my workstation and jogged out the back and into the car park, where I knew I wouldn't be overheard.

She answered her phone. Must have been a free period or something.

'I was just about to call you, Kevin.'

'Look, Max, I hope you don't mind me asking—'

'I've already spoken to the witness.'

'You have? How'd he sound?'

'His English is terrible.'

'So what? He's not at your school.'

'Kevin, what I was going to say is, would you pick me up at half past six? You know the lay of the land and I would appreciate the support.'

'I'm relieved, Lead Investigator. This looks like it could be it.'

'Let's keep this between ourselves. I don't want to involve Derek at the moment. He distracts the witnesses.'

'But he's got special skills.' The Funnel should have been in on this. You can't exclude a hardcore Knower, not in the GIT.

'We can talk about this later.'

'Yeah, okay. Loose lips sink ships, as they say.'

'Precisely. Except there's more chance we'll find a ship on his lawn than an apeman in Sutton. Bye.'

> • <

The existence of an 'apeman' in Sutton might seem incongruous, or even ridiculous. It's beyond the realms of possibility that a gigantic ape-like biped could be living among us in the London Borough of Sutton. It's too incredible that a dirty great species of huge hairy giants, evolutionary throwbacks to a nobler age, could live undetected in a built-up area on the edge of one of the world's noisiest cities. FACT: Sutton has been a hotspot for sightings for years, if not centuries. The people of Sutton have been catching glimpses of the 'Long Man' for a very long time. Most of them don't like to talk about it, in case they get locked up under the Mental Health Act.

This is where the GIT comes in. We're like the fifth emergency service. No one thinks they need us until they've seen something in the woods they can't explain.

There have always been stories (aka The Lore). Like, FACT: according to Derek Funnel, during the reign of Edward VI, the lord of the manor, D'Arcy of Cliche, kept a 'grate ape' in a stable on his lands until peasants burned it at the stake for being a Spanish spy; and in the nineteenth century, navvies building the London-to-Sutton railway kept seeing a 'furry devilman' watching them from a ridge with red, glowing eyes. But the first *audio-visual* evidence of Giganto occurred in 1988, when on 31 March, legendary investigator Eddie Gartree, known in our fraternity as 'Gorgo', and his mate Jackie Hogg, the men who started it all, the original men with kit, filmed one as it passed through Sutton Cock crossroads. This is the Holy Grail, north Surrey's answer to the 1967 Patterson-Gimlin film. In Patterson-Gimlin, a

Bigfoot is caught out in the open in Bluff Creek, California. It was a female one. You can see her bosoms move around in a way that would be impossible to fake.

Ever since I first saw the Patterson-Gimlin film on *Arthur C. Clarke's Mysterious World* when I was a kid, I was a Believer. That moment. Seeing the majestic figure with her distinctive arm swings and tit-shiver lope across those logs, the imperious turn of her cone-shaped head as she looks back at us. This was luminous to me. It was like finding God. My mum always talked about helping me find God, but it was not her that led me to God. It was Arthur C. The sparkle on the glass skull in the title sequence of *Mysterious World*: that was the bright light of heaven to me. The title music was like a Bontempi organ version of *Thus Sprake Zarathustra* from *2001: A Space Odyssey* (which – fuck me – Arthur C. also wrote). It sounded like the soundtrack of God to me back then.

Still does now, I have to admit.

I never knew my father. Whoever he is, or was, Mum kept silent about him to the grave. If I asked, she only ever said that Jesus would have to do. Jesus was enough. Knowing what she was like, I don't dwell on how I came about, I don't like to go there. But when I thought about my dad – whenever I thought of how my dad would have let me read the fanciful things, would have bought me the Ladybird *Dracula* – I hoped my real dad, the one who wasn't Jesus, was like – or was actually – Arthur C. Clarke, curator of earthly mysteries. When I saw the Patterson-Gimlin film on *Arthur C. Clarke's Mysterious World* and listened to all his theories about it, I knew. I knew I was going to be an adventurer in search of answers to difficult questions from then on in. I am proud that I have become the sort of person I imagined myself to be when I was eight.

Derek Funnel's moment of revelation came from a memory of the yeti that stalks the London Underground in *Doctor Who and the Web of Fear*, but, FACT, this was broadcast before he was born and five of the episodes have been mysteriously lost. Sci-Borg reckons he might just have read the Terrence Dicks book version of it that you could get in all the libraries when we were kids and it frakked him right up.

If *Arthur C. Clarke's Mysterious World* made me a Believer, it wasn't until I saw the Gartree-Hogg film of 1988 that I became a Knower.

> • <

The story goes that just after closing time on the evening of 31 March, Gartree and Hogg left the Buffers pub opposite Sutton Station and headed down the high street towards the crossroads known locally as The Cock.

As they approached The Cock, they spotted a large figure crouching behind some bins. Hogg later described himself as being 'shat up' by the sight. Gartree estimated that he was about eighteen feet away from the figure and spent about ten seconds retrieving his cine camera from his bag (he worked for a regional TV news programme and always had a small cine camera about his person).

The figure then walked away from the bins and crossed the road. The resulting film (about twenty seconds long) is initially all over the shop, as Gartree struggles to keep the camera level. The film stabilises after about fifteen seconds. Here, the figure turns and looks back, revealing its disturbing red eyes.

At this point, Hogg fell to his knees and 'pantsed himself'. Hogg – a very large man, an ex-paratrooper and rugby prop forward not easily intimidated – would later tell me that it wasn't Giganto's red eyes or its horrible smell that did him in, but its expression of 'serene and inhuman indifference'.

Soon after looking over its shoulder, the creature disappeared into the alleyway that led to Carats nightclub and a minicab office. Bouncers at Carats that night and a Mrs Maureen Lambey, who worked in the cab office, both reported glimpsing a 'weirdo' or 'tall bloke' in the vicinity.

The footage was shown on Gorgo's regional news programme. Then, the government and the mainstream media hushed it up. I'd seen it, though – and as soon as I saw it, Kevin Stubbs, Hardcore Knower, was born.

This was no hoax. I don't care what Sci-Borg says, the Gartree-Hogg footage is not a hoax, FACT. And anyway, none of that was important now. Today we had new footage that, even though we hadn't seen it yet, would prove there was a gigantopithecus in northern Surrey – in Sutton, to be precise – and it had been here forever.

Out in the car park, after I'd hung up on Sci-Borg, I thought it all through and allowed myself to dream for once. In my mind, I assembled the kit. I rehearsed it all.

The moment we confirmed the truth captured in that film.

The moment we released it to the press and changed everything.

The moment we turned all of science on its head.

The moment she would have me back.

The moment I told my boy and his eyes lit up with respect and wonder again.

The moment we were reunited in the forests of north Surrey.

GIGANTOPITHECUS INTELLIGENCE TEAM

REPORT #214 (CATEGORY A)

SECTION 2

OBSERVED:

Me and my girlfriend, Summer, had taken our kids to the Common. It was Kyla, our eldest's, ninth birthday and we had decided to have a barbecue outside where we could play some tunes and get out of it. My mate Dawkers had come along with his girlfriend Maddiaon and her kids. My girlfriend's mate from her work had come too, with her kids and some bloke, and some of the geezers from The Churn with their kids and their girlfriends. In all, there must have been about fifty of us. We had a barbie going and some banging tunes. The little girls were dancing up and down in lines, cute like, and even some of the grown-ups were having a bit of an old-school rave. We were on this flat bit of grass. About twenty yards away was trees. Everything was normal until about nine o'clock. The moon had come out and the light was starting to go in.

I got my mobile out so I could film Kyla doing her moves. Anyway, I have the camera on her and it's recording and everything when I hear Dawkers shout out, 'What the f***'s that?' I look up and I see this, well, this big thing standing in the trees. It was bigger than one of those basketball players you get in the States. It had a triangle for a head. It was just standing there but you could see its eyes. They were red and they glowed. Dawkers goes to me, 'There's a f****** paedo in them woods.' But what I saw weren't no paedo. It was just standing there, staring at me and my mates.

I lifted up my mobile and then it must have noticed or something, because it started to run along the line of the trees. Now, right, all the kids and the women saw it and they all started to scream. It was like something out of *Jaws*, the way they were yelling. I had the camera trained on it. It was black and hairy, wider and bigger than a normal person and it had no neck and you could see its red eyes glow as it swayed through the trees. It weren't clumsy or nothing. It kind of moved like I reckon a ninja might move. I could see its arms and its legs. Its arms looked well long.

We were all about twenty yards from it when it ran off towards the golf course. Kyla came up to me and said, 'Daddy, what the f*** was that?' I was shocked she had seen such a horrible thing.

I can't deny what we saw. I have to say that, because it was real.

Summer saw it too, when it was standing there and when it was running. So did Dawkers, Maddiaon, Kyla, Dojo, Sammy Lee, Jade, Rami, Dylan Parker-Prince, Morgan the Aussie, and Bobby Meakle, and he runs the Chicago Rock. Me and Dawkers and Sammy and Bobby Meakle went up there after it but we couldn't find no tracks or nothing. The ground was tough under the trees, but we did find some dog mess and a mouldy porn mag under a bush. It was getting dark by now and the women and kids were freaked, so we took them home. We agreed to come back the next day for a proper look about, but to be honest we bricked it and went down The Churn.

I reckon it was quite smart and didn't want to be seen, and if Dawkers hadn't called it a paedo it would have just waited there until we packed it in. That's why it didn't say nothing. It must have known what we would have done if we reckoned there was a paedo in the woods watching the kiddies.

If someone else was telling me this, I'd reckon they were mental or caned. But it's me telling this, and I have all of it, the whole malarkey, on my phone.

REPORT #214:
THE FACTS BY KEVIN STUBBS:
SECTION TWO

When I got back to my flat (which I used to refer to as 'Knower's Ark', for a laugh), I took my first real opportunity to go over what Clive at work would call the 'granulars' of Report #214. The first thing I noticed is that the way the witness described the creature conforms to the majority of sightings:

Gigantic
Hairy
Long, swinging arms
Red, glowing eyes
Cone-shaped cranium

Basically, if you've seen something like this, and you live in north Surrey, the only explanation is that you've seen the North Surrey Gigantopithecus.

What else is it going to be?

It's not going to be a bear, is it? The gigantopithei wiped out the English bears in the Middle Ages, a cataclysmic event that Derek Funnel researched in detail and added to The Lore in the appendix to Report #138: The Third Canonical Sighting of The Purley Way Wendigo. Derek Funnel has always been a professionalizing influence on the GIT, and helped us add cultural depth to our report writing. It was itching my unmentionables that Sci-Borg wanted to exclude him from what could well be the Great Confirmation.

I wished it was just me and The Funnel on this op, and Gorgo. Gorgo should have been with us on this one, not her. Or, I should have been in charge. Gorgo should never have put her in charge when he left.

There was, though, this matter of honour called 'chain of command' in the GIT, so I was duty-bound to do as she ordered. This was stressing me out, I have to admit.

I locked myself in the bathroom and did some breathing exercises to calm myself down. When they did nothing for me, I tried some of the Tibetan meditation techniques The Funnel had taught me, but knowing I was about to screw him over made it worse. Eventually, I allowed myself to stare at my face in the bathroom mirror and mentally reminded myself what we were doing here and what was about to happen. It didn't matter whether we did it her way or my way. The Great Confirmation was nigh. Nigh meant soon. It also meant that imminently, no one – not Sci-Borg, not Boho and not my boy – could ask me to change, because I'd been right all along.

> • <

There had been a time when my boy believed in this thing of mine. When he was born, because I'd made a solemn promise to Boho, I gave up the GIT, the expeditions, the camping, the staying up all night, the weekly team discussion evenings in The Churn. Before he was born was one of the best periods of my life. Not only had I pulled for once, but these were also what I called the GIT Supreme days of the classic line-up (Me, Kevin Stubbs, aka Agent MonkeyMagic; Edward 'Eddie' Gartree, aka Gorgo, The Man Who Started It All;

and Derek Funnel, aka The Funnel). When I got married I left them to it. They became what I called Continuity GIT. I had every intention of leaving it alone, of being a proper dad and a husband and all that, now that I had a kid and my wife's English was good enough for us to actually have a conversation that wasn't like a game of charades or moving ships about using semaphore. I am not saying I didn't hanker. I'm not saying I forgot. I'm not saying I didn't feel forlorn and wistful when I smelled crisp autumn air or pine needles.

When he was old enough, I formed a little GIT fun team. It was perhaps my favourite of all the teams. It was like GIT Cubs, just my boy and me.

On Saturday evenings we would drive out into the woods, a cool-box added to the usual kit, and sit up all night in the van: Oaks Park, Chaldon trig point, Reigate Hill, Box Hill, Raynes Park, all the hotspots. I'd explain The Lore, passing it down from father to son. There would be tea in a flask and sandwiches I'd cut up nice and small, and a Wagon Wheel each.

These were the perfect moments for me. Not all I'd ever wanted, but something nearly as good as seeing a gigantopithecus rampant. Nearly as good as seeing a gigantopithecus was the first time I saw Kyrylo wrapped up in a white blanket and cradled in Boho's arms, her sitting up in the hospital bed and her smile then. That first time he gripped my thumb with his little fist. The look of joy on his face when he puffed out all four candles on his birthday cake at once and the three of us all blew the lingering smoke away and collapsed into laughing. When we took the stabilisers off the bike and he rode away from me for the first time without falling over. I wanted us to build on these memories in the woods, on stake-out operations in the van. I wanted him to have childhood memories of me that I did not have with my old man. We would watch out for it together, and in doing so we would be together forever.

I thought he liked it. I would have liked it, when I was his age. My mum didn't even let me go outside on my own. And she only encouraged me to keep my mind closed by making me read about Jesus over and over again as if he were a real person who could spring out from behind the curtains at any time. I didn't have an old man to take me out in the woods and into the Great Spaces. While we were out in the van, just me and my boy, gigantopithecus spotting, I often thought that if I'd known my dad he would have taken me out like this. He would have shown me how to read shadows and scat, how to do a wood knock and a 'squatch call, things I'd had to learn from Gorgo. My dad, who I sometimes thought of as Arthur C. Dad, would have passed down The Lore to me, so when I'd seen the Gartree-Hogg footage for the first time I would have been properly prepared and not so shat up. I wished Arthur C. Dad had taken me out into the woods to show me the grand and noble ones. Instead, at weekends, I'd often found myself sitting in some side-room with *The Watchtower* or *The Silver Chair* while Mum was in a Bible study group in some Kingdom Hall somewhere in Sutton or south London or Surrey. Occasionally, this was made even more boring by having to sit in some weirdo's house with the shy, frakked-up kids of other Witnesses while Mum and their parents talked about whatever they hated the most that week: vaccines, voting, VD, whatever. I didn't want any of that cold empty bollocks for my boy. I wanted him to live, to Know. What I didn't want was for him to ever find himself in some conservatory in New Malden with an eight-year-old girl called Ruth whose idea of play was to ask, 'Kevin, have you considered your relationship with the risen Christ?' Arthur C. Dad wouldn't have let that happen to me. I wasn't going to let that happen to my boy.

His eight birthday was on a Saturday. He was born in June, so it was warm, summer, a great time for his old man to take him out squatching. That night we were parked up on Chipstead Downs, but no sooner had we arrived he drifted off in the passenger seat. I was drawing a blanket around him when I heard something outside. Truth be told, I didn't hear it. I sensed it vibrate through nature, quiver in the night air. My boy was asleep. Zonked out. Dead to the world. I put on my night-vision goggles and slid out into the darkness. I could definitely hear its Darth-Vader-like breathing. I could smell its horrible smell, too.

You're not supposed to see it. It's not supposed to exist. It can scare the bollocks off you. Just look what happened to Jackie Hogg, one of the Original Knowers. In the early days of GIT, pre the arrival on the scene of the young believer Kevin Stubbs, Jackie had seen Giganto so often that his nerves unravelled. It was like he'd been playing a horror-based role-playing game where the characters have a sanity score. I'd played one of these on a rainy Sunday afternoon round Derek Funnel's flat on the Poet's Estate with some of his UFO nutter mates from Caterham. It was like Jackie had actually been living in one of these games. Every time he'd seen Giganto, he'd rolled a twenty-sided die and whatever number came up had been deducted from his mind. I'm not like that. I am solid.

I had my back to the van and Giganto was in the trees. I could hear him. I could certainly smell him. I could smell, too, that he was moving off. Also, his breathing was not as loud as it had been. Using my ninja stealth skills, and with camera at the ready, I followed. I didn't intend to be gone long, only a few minutes, tops.

All the time it was ahead of me, an outline in the trees, crisscrossed by fronds: a brown giant, more shadow than man. As the sun came up, just for a second, as I scrambled towards it, I knew that I had it, that it was here in the forests, something that would one day hold out an understanding hand, that would help me be a man of his world, a citizen of eternal nature. But it vanished, and I was left standing with nothing but the woods and the feeling that one day soon we would see each other again.

Boho was right that I was a frakker not to think ahead. That our boy might well wake up in the van, in the dark, on his own in an isolated spot I'd convinced him was like a prehistoric glade where ten-foot-tall ape-bipeds with cone-shaped heads still roamed and roared, that could shred a deer to pieces and, it was theorised, were attracted by the smell of Wagon Wheels (see Report #181: The Stalker of the Wilderness).

The thing is, when you're a kid, adventure is all in the mind. It's not real. It all happens under controlled circumstances: supervision, teachers, mind control, thought police. This just isn't so when you're a grown man, a Knower. I tried to tell myself and Boho that that was what I was trying to communicate to him, that in my own way I was trying to show him the real world.

Anyway, she didn't want to hear any of that. That was the end of us, me and her. She demanded that I stop going out looking for Giganto, and when I didn't say 'of course' straightaway I was out of the house. I was sleeping in my van. I was not allowed back until I admitted it wasn't real. But it was real, I'd seen it loads of times.

Even after I was granted access, I wasn't allowed to take him out into the woods anymore. We only did miserable shitty things you're allowed to do with kids on weekends, like eat junk and watch bollocks.

By then, the classic line-up had reformed. Continuity GIT was no more, GIT Supreme was back doing our reunion tour of Sutton and north Surrey: Gorgo, MonkeyMagic and The Funnel, not just revisiting the hits but recording new material as well. I was back in the GIT. I belonged again. I was really happy. I was really sad. I missed them both, Boho and my boy. It was confusing.

When he started proper school, I don't know, the other kids would say their dads knew me or knew of me, of this thing of mine. I don't know what they said about me, but I can guess. Soon my boy didn't want to see me either, unless I stopped going on about Giganto.

This had me in a frenzy of decision-making for six days. It would have been the easiest thing in the world to go into denial, to stop going on about the Gigantopithecus, to move on with life, get back with my boy, show him other things like the other dads, football and rubbish, slide back in with my wife, be Domestic Kev again. But I couldn't. I'd seen it loads of times. It's real. As real as he is. As real as they are.

What sort of message would I be giving out if I tell him to ignore the great wonder of life just to fit in with small-minded dickheads – and dickheads from Sutton, the worst kind of dickheads.

The thing is: come the Great Confirmation, Giganto is the only thing that anyone will be going on about, and my boy will become the proud son of the hero-adventurer who turned all of science on its head.

> • <

Now sure of what I was doing, I let myself out of the bathroom. I made a call, kitted up, and went out to the official GIT van, aka the Abominable Snowmobile. I gunned the engine and bombed round to Sci-Borg's flat.

GIGANTOPITHECUS INTELLIGENCE TEAM

REPORT #214 (CATEGORY A)

SECTION 3

Initial Follow-up Investigation by GIT Lead Investigator Maxine Cash.

I spoke with this witness on the telephone on 8 July.

It was dusk when the witnesses saw the cryptid. The cryptid is said to have paused in the nearby trees. It moved once it realised it was being observed. From a distance of some twenty yards, in half-light, it was assumed that the cryptid was covered in dark brown hair. It moved like a person but with an animal swiftness. The cryptid may have been seen by a large group of people, up to fifty, which is unusual in such cases. Men from the group investigated the scene but found no tracks or unusual marks on the trees.

This area is the most northerly of four separate areas of land known as Banstead Commons. It is two kilometres south of Sutton, and close to the A217, known as the Brighton Road. To the west of the Common is the Banstead Downs Golf Course. The surrounding area is largely residential and densely populated.

Although there have been a series of recent category C and B reports originating from this area (tree-knocks, vocalisations, reports of 'eye shine' and a putrid smell in the woods, plus the repeated late-night disturbance caused to dogs in nearby Belmont), the ecology equation in what is a suburban district does not suggest that a large bipedal hominid could subsist in the area.

It would seem that most of the witnesses were either children or under the influence of alcohol and recreational drugs. The light was poor and from a distance of twenty yards what they thought they saw could have been a large man. This could also be a classic case of pareidolia: a trick of the light, given shape and substance only by individual perception and the desire in the viewer to see something significant. It is also possible that this is another hoax, as in the cases of the 'Worcester Park Yeti', 'the Cheam Monster', 'the Ape-Beast of Carshalton Beeches' and the 'Nonsuch Kong'.

However, as the witness claimed to have filmed the sighting, I instigated a further investigation by the Gigantopithecus Intelligence Team.

REPORT #214:
THE FACTS BY KEVIN STUBBS:
SECTION THREE

On the night of the first investigation into Report #214, I parked the Abominable outside Sci-Borg's flat. When she finally made an appearance, she was wearing her field-trip garb – a pistachio-green Lycra cycling costume with black flashes, and sunglasses shaped like swimming goggles.

She clambered into the Abominable.

'Hiya, Kevin. How have you been feeling? Been drinking the camomile tea I gave you?'

'Nah. Tastes like pot pourri—'

'I hope you haven't been getting overexcited this afternoon.'

'No, I've been frosty. Been trying to be like you said. Not jump to any conclusions. Wait till I've seen the evidence before I think it's evidence.'

'We'll make a scientist of you yet.'

'Does that mean, shut up and drive?'

'Yes.'

I gunned the van and drove off. Every now and again I tried to check her face in the mirror. Meanwhile, I ran through the six main things she had tried to teach me.

One: Extraordinary claims require extraordinary evidence.

Two: For a theory to be meaningful you have to be able to falsify it.

Three: The simpler explanation is liable to be the one that counts.

Four: You need to be able to repeat a claim over and over again.

Five: Make sure you can kick to the kerb any other ideas on a subject.

Six: A correlation between two things doesn't prove a connection between them.

I was also thinking that at the end of *Arthur C. Clarke's Mysterious World* about the Missing Apes, when he says that Patty in the Paterson-Gimlin film is probably fake because the *2001* film that he wrote proves you can make convincing ape-like biped costumes, he was wrong, because those *2001* monkey costumes now look bollocks and Patty still looks awesome. He's having a giraffe with us, anyway. Arthur C. was a Knower, FACT. Pretending we didn't know what we knew in front of civilians and sheeple was what Gorgo had taught us to do. He probably copied it from Arthur C.

About five minutes later, Sci-Borg said, 'Kevin, we're going the wrong way.'

'We're picking up The Funnel.'

'We are not. I was very explicit in my instructions.'

'He knew what was going on. He's like that.'

'Cancel him.'

'Wouldn't be right, not now.'

'I'll call him, then.'

'You can't stand him down now.'

'I'm Lead Investigator. Of course I can.'

'We need his skills.'

'We do not. He's a dangerous fantasist.'

'He's a legend.'

'No, he's not.'

'Yes, he is.'

I didn't change course, kept heading towards The Funnel's place on the Poet's Estate.

> • <

Derek Funnel is a legend in this tight-knit confraternity of men with kit from Sutton who seek out the gigantopithecus. Not a lot is known about his daytime activities, except he works in Waterstone's in Sutton. I've only been to his flat a couple of times. It's fortified, as you'd expect: grilles on the windows, a reinforced front door, pentagrams chalked on the step. Inside, it's part wizard's tower, part spooky library from one of those Cthulhu books he gave me to read that have no story and long words. There's a shrine and a big portrait of some bald bloke who The Funnel says had a lot to say about the gigantopithecus before the war. The blinds are constantly drawn. They come at night, he says.

This is one of the great things about getting involved in the GIT. You meet people you wouldn't ordinarily meet, if you just did your day job in IT support and knocked about in The Churn and The Dog. Left to my own devices, I wouldn't be seen dead with someone who looks like Derek Funnel. If you can imagine some hippy-dippy, love-in, prog-jazz West German experimental music commune from the seventies, and fronting them a stunted, barrel-chested, flute-playing Mr Tumnus, then you've had a Category B sighting of The Funnel.

Every gigantopithecus team needs someone like Derek Funnel, even though the ManBeast GB research group gave him the brush off, and Hominid Rex wouldn't let him join them because they're a Jamiroquai tribute band.

Derek Funnel is a paranormal investigator and cryptozoologist. If you check out his website – *thegreatbeast* – you'll see there isn't anything on Earth that he says he hasn't investigated. He has done ghosts and poltergeists; big cats and hellhounds; black-eyed children, The Rake, and the man with a pig's head that haunts the Black Country. He spent his twenties trying to prove categorically that UFOs are real; he's seen a yeti in Nepal, the batutat in Vietnam, the orang pendek in Sumatra, and he says he once sat down in a clearing by Lake Baikal and shared a dead salmon with an Alma, a Central Asian cousin of the North Surrey Gigantopithecus.

He'd first got wind of the North Surrey Gigantopithecus when years ago, apparently, a bloke in Sutton told another bloke in Sutton who told Derek Funnel that a bloke had seen a 'blue movie' (aka a porn film) in which former British Prime Minister Edward Heath was shagging a juvenile gigantopithecus, and at the end Edward Heath transformed into a massive orange lizard-man thing and then he took us into the EEC, aka the EU.

I don't think this film is canon yet. He thinks it is, and he says he has gone to extraordinary lengths to find the tape.

After that investigation hit a brick wall, though, he says he spent seven years hunting Mokele-Mbembe, the real dinosaur that lives in the Congo. He reckons he proved that, came back to Sutton, got a job in Waterstone's, and came straight to us. Well, straight to us via ManBeast GB and Hominid Rex.

Under his pen name – Tom Egatherion – he has also written

a stack of proper books that you actually buy on the Internet: *Dark They Were with Red Glowing Eyes: The Search for Britain's Bigfoot*; *The Man-Monkey Mystery: Phase/Cloak/Prophecy*; *A Memorex for the Kraken*; and *White Stains, Great Beast: The North Surrey Gigantopithecus and I*.

I did disagree – gently, of course – with The Funnel's theory that the North Surrey Gigantopithecus was a supernatural being from another dimension that used advanced cloaking technology to move unseen among us. He says that nothing natural would have red glowing eyes. I don't agree, and neither does Gorgo. The North Surrey Gigantopithecus is part of us, part of evolutionary history, the missing link.

That Piltdown Man they dug up in Piltdown in 1912? That wasn't a hoax. It was a gigantopithecus, FACT.

I'm a specialist naturalist – perhaps with more in common with Sci-Borg than she'd like to admit – and The Funnel is a paranormal cryptozoologist. You need that sort of debate and tension within a team. You need alternative viewpoints, the beautiful melting pot of competing ideas out of which only one true Knowing will emerge.

> • <

When I pulled up the Abominable outside The Funnel's place, and just as I was about to sling back the sliding door, Sci-Borg grabbed hold of my arm.

'What do you actually know about Derek?'

'Enough,' I said.

'He doesn't work in Waterstone's. He says he does, but he doesn't.'

'I've *seen* him in Waterstone's.'

'I rang Derek at the shop the other day, because he wasn't answering his mobile, and they'd never heard of him. Never heard of someone called Derek Funnel. You think you'd remember if you'd met someone called Derek Funnel, wouldn't you? Especially *this* Derek Funnel. I even spelled that out. You'd remember him. Eccentric dresser. Distinct way of speaking. A taste for the exotic.'

'They have a high turnover in those places. It's basically a KFC for books.'

'I did some digging, and I found something that creeped me out.'

'Listen, you need to pull yourself together. Not long from now, you're going to see something that will *massively* creep you out.'

'I think he's a devotee of Aleister Crowley.'

'What has that got to do with anything?'

'I think we need to be prepared for the fact that Derek's research CV is a fabrication designed to conceal some other agenda.'

'C'mon, Max,' I said. 'Gorgo and Jackie did all these psychometric tests when we met The Funnel, all these background checks and psychology profiles. Jackie was in the paras.'

'I'm not sure he was, Kevin.'

'Jackie could smell a wrong 'un a mile away. And you know how many spanners and lunatics want to be in on this thing of ours? We don't let just anyone in.'

At this point, The Funnel appeared at his front door, the breeze rippling his bell-bottoms and the fronds of his hair. There was a bulge in his trench-coat pocket, but I knew what that was: his electromagnetic field reader (aka the Trifield 100XE, a great bit of kit; aka The Tractor Beam). I have to admit that I felt a lot happier all of a sudden. It was as if the natural excitement I should have been feeling, the passion that Sci-Borg was trying to dampen, flooded through me. When I saw The Funnel prance up his path towards us, it was like when I was a kid, and I met other kids who were not drokked-up-already Witness kids: I got so excited I scared the others, I was so lit-up and happy. I felt like that.

He got into the van and sat behind us.

'Good evening, Stubbs. Maxine, hail. Hail, Maxine, and I hope you don't think it improper but I've been lounging around all afternoon wondering if you'd read Gustav Meyrink's *The German Neanderthal's Magic Horn*?'

'The title's a bit of a mouthful,' she said. 'I'm surprised you can remember it.'

'*The Magic Horn*,' said The Funnel, 'is a far richer text than *The Golem*—'

'What?' I said. 'Gollum wrote a book?'

'It's a Jewish fairy tale,' said Maxine. 'Meyrick wrote a modernist rendering of—'

'I'm having you on, Lead Investigator. You think I'd seriously believe that Gollum could write a book? He's bollock-naked, and he lives down a cave.'

'Why would I not think that you'll believe anything, Kevin?'

The Funnel stuck his oar in. 'A wise man once said that everyone interprets everything in terms of his own experience.'

'Yeah,' I said. 'I've seen it loads of times. You've seen it loads of times. We've seen it loads of times—'

'Right, you two,' said Sci-Borg, 'let's lay down some team ground rules for tonight's investigation—'

'I'm assuming, Del,' I said, 'that the German Neanderthal is their version of the Long Man, and his magic horn is his—?'

'The uniform of its imagery doth perhaps slink through the pages—'

'Gentlemen, please be quiet. I want us to focus on tonight's investigation. Now, I know you must be excited—'

'Excited? Del, you excited?'

'I feel the Death card is in play.'

'We're not going to kill it. We're not the Home Office—'

'Guys, please, focus. We'll be more excited when we have proper proof, but I need you – especially you, Kevin – I need you both to prepare yourselves for the eventuality that there's nothing on that film.'

'Given the ellipticality of mirror-world objects,' said The Funnel, 'faith may well be our spirit barometer—'

'Focus, please. All I am saying here is that, yes, we need to see the film, but come prepared with a healthy dose of scepticism—'

'May I suggest, Lead Investigator,' said The Funnel, 'that you and I perhaps stress scepticism in different ways. For me, I think it's what we select to be sceptical of.'

'Derek, use the method I've set down: L.R.C.R. Listen. Record. Collect. Reflect.'

'That's just management speak, that is,' I said. 'You can only say it if you've never had a Category A encounter with a gigantopithecus in northern Surrey.'

'Which you haven't, Kevin. They're extinct.'

'I've seen it, load of times, since I was eighteen. Saw it rampant in Morden Cemetery, me and Gorgo, the Original

Knower. Saw it. In the trees. Rampant. Gigantic. Cone-shaped. The lot.'

'*Say* you saw it. No proof. Do you want me to go over the six points again, especially the first one?'

'Saw it with the evidence of my own eyes the next time, out with Gorgo, outside St Helier's Hospital on Wrythe Green Lane. Gigantic, hairy, long swinging arms. I saw it. Gorgo saw it.'

'Edward Gartree—'

'Gorgo. It's Gorgo. We're in the field. Field names only.'

'Field names only? I don't have a field name.'

We looked at each other, The Funnel and me, and sniggered. Sometimes the only good thing about Maxine being Lead Investigator and not knowing that behind her back we called her Sci-Borg and Lego Helmet Hair and The Cakaleta Teapot – that's Nepali for The Chocolate Teapot – was that sometimes it had the same atmosphere it had at school, when the supply teacher was a woman who looked like an elephant or a vampire or Elton John how he looked in 1974, or that Steve Interesting Davis, the snooker player, and she'd lose control of the class and everyone went mental until some bald PE teacher came in and started shouting the shit out of everyone.

'Edward Gartree, Gargamel, Gormo or whatever you insist on calling him,' said Sci-Borg, 'he's quite a character. All I am saying is that you and Edward Gartree saying you saw something a long time ago when you were probably drunk is not science.'

'It is, though,' said The Funnel, 'religion.'

'Lead Investigator, you weren't there when me and Gorgo recorded the now legendary Hackbridge Howl on the Sci-Bionic Parabolic Microphone—'

'I've heard that audio, Kevin. It's foxes mating.'

'It is not.'

'It is.'

'How can you say that was two foxes having it off?'

'Because it is.'

'It isn't,' said Derek. 'It's the sound they emit when they come out of phase.'

'It isn't.'

'And I won't bollock on about any of them now,' I said, 'but the Worcester Park Yeti, the Cheam Monster, the Ape-Beast of Carshalton Beeches and the Nonsuch Kong were one hundred per cent cast-iron Giganto sightings, FACT, and they shouldn't be disrespected out of hand. If you're not a Knower, you shouldn't be in charge here, should you?'

'You know that's not why I'm here, Kevin. I know there's no monster. I'm doing this to help you in other ways. Drive. Let's get on with this. Put your foot down. And both of you, no monkey business in this man's house. There are children there.'

I knew I needed to calm down now. I did know, I promise.

GIGANTOPITHECUS INTELLIGENCE TEAM

REPORT #214 (CATEGORY A)

SECTION 4

Report on Field Trip, 08/7

<u>GIT Investigators</u>

Lead Investigator: Maxine Cash
Secondary Investigator: Kevin Stubbs
Cryptozoologist: Derek Funnel

There was some confusion as to how the team was to organise for the investigation.

REPORT #214:
THE FACTS BY KEVIN STUBBS:
SECTION FOUR

It must be obvious from what I have reported so far that Maxine was totally the wrong person to be in charge of the Gigantopithecus Intelligence Team. You must have been asking yourself how did she become Lead Investigator when Gorgo retired, and not someone more qualified, like me or The Funnel. The Funnel – well, despite claiming to be a prophet sometimes and that he has memories of knocking about with pharaohs and goddesses, and climbing yeti mountains between the wars, he's more of a librarian type, like Giles out of *Buffy the Vampire Slayer* but with a rascal barnet. I was the more likely candidate.

The reason the honour fell to her had nothing to do with me screwing up, and everything to do with Boho. It was Boho who jump-started the fatal mechanism that started to turn the crankshafts that kicked over a ball bearing that ran down some rickety plastic stairs and along a snaking tube and jogged another ball off a high-up bath with a hole in it, that fell onto the end of a diving board that sent a little plastic man spinning into a tub, who in the end caused a red cage to drop over me and allowed Maxine to swan in and become the Lead Investigator of the GIT.

> • <

Maxine teaches science at the school where Boho sends my boy, Kyrylo. Right, that's not my idea of a good name for a kid who is going to have to hold his own in a town on the edge of civilisation like Sutton. Anyway, Kyrylo is what he's called *legally*. It was a massive problem between me and Boho, the first big problem we really had. I did want to make her happy but I also wanted to call our boy Tarzan. I used to love that *Tarzan, Lord of the Jungle* cartoon when I was a kid. I only saw it a couple of times, always round other people's houses, of course. I especially liked the bit about being adopted by a kindly she-ape named Kala, and 'This is my domain', and that *ahraaararaahhhhhhh-hah* he used to do that I later adopted as a 'squatch call to draw Giganto out of the woods. No one's called names like Kevin nowadays; it's all Zoro and Pacman and Skype. Tarzan Stubbs would have been well this century.

So, we had a big bust-up about the name, me and Boho. She says 'Tarzan' sounds Arab or Tartar to her. She's not having it. She's massively unreasonable about it as well, and the poor little mite gets lumbered with Kyrylo. He doesn't even get Tarzan as a second name, or Kevin.

One day last year, I'm at work, setting up email accounts for new iiSkipper pod droids or something, when Boho rings me up.

'Kevin, are you sat down on your arse in gear?' Sometimes I really wished someone else had taught her how to speak English instead of me. Boho is from the Ukraine. When we married, she couldn't speak English at all, apart from 'yes', 'no', and for some reason, 'Do you believe in life after love.' How we met is a long, complicated story of found-footage, pop-up ads, fat fingers, Old Speckled Hen, desperation, aspiration, migration, marriage agencies, interpreters, misinterpreters and meetings in airports that really needs someone with the talent of Arthur C. Dad to make sense of and decipher.

'You're not standing up behind tree?' she said. 'Sometimes I bell and you are standing behind tree, or you say you cannot talk because you are standing behind tree. How am I to know that you are not standing behind tree—'

'It's the middle of the day?'

'It's Kyrylo. The school bell me up. They say Kyrylo, his behaviour is disturbed. I tried to tell them about you, but they want me to go and see them, and they want me to bring you with me. I said you might be standing behind a tree like nutjobperson, but—'

> • <

At the school, Boho is already sat in a classroom with this prim-and-proper lady with long arms and dippy glasses. I had a word with myself and told myself to be on my best behaviour, just like I do at work when I have to deal with people like Clive.

'I'm really sorry to ask you both to come in like this,' she said. 'This is never nice, I know, but I do need to bring to your attention that over the last six months or so we've noticed a marked deterioration in Kyrylo's grades, but more recently his behaviour—'

'Well, it's obvious why,' I said. 'He needs a grounding influence. He needs to spend more time with his dad—'

Boho turned to me. 'Kevin, *he* does not want to see *you*. *He* says so.'

'Recently,' said Ms Cash, 'he's been sullen, surly, disagreeable, distracted and he's been involved in three fights with groups of other boys—'

'That's normal in Sutton,' I said.

'That shouldn't be the case, Mr Stubbs. Now, here's the difficult bit. This is why I've asked you to come in and not yet actioned any sort of disciplinary procedure against Kyrylo. We do not tolerate violent conduct at this school, but when I spoke to Kyrylo he said his father – I assume he means you, Mr Stubbs – spends all his free time looking for a local "Bigfoot" style animal and is so widely known for it that the other boys are mercilessly ribbing Kyrylo. That's why he's lashing out. I assume this is not the case, but I thought I'd better consult with you both first.'

'It's not true,' I said.

'Oh dear,' said Ms Cash. 'We may have a more pressing problem than just the fighting. Parents separating can have a profound effect on a young person—'

'It's not a "Bigfoot-*style* animal",' I said. 'It's a gigantopithecus.'

Boho burst into tears. 'It is true. He is always believing there are the big monkeys in Sutton.'

'How many times? It is not a monkey.'

'He did not tell me this before we met, that he believes there are the big monkeys in Sutton—'

'A monkey's got a frakking tail. It's an ape—'

'I don't care if it is monkey or ape. It is not right. You, Kevin, sneaking around at night with electrical things and bonkerspersons looking for big monkeys in Sutton. And then writing bollocks on website so everyone in Sutton can read it, and now it is not funny anymore as children are reading it and laughing at Kyrylo.'

'But I've seen it loads of times,' I said. 'I want him to come out with me. I want him to Know—'

Boho turns to Ms Cash. 'For the life of my son. You are a lady of methods. Please, prove to *him* that these monkeys are not real.'

'For crying out loud—'

'Mr Stubbs,' said Ms Cash, 'no such animal can exist here in Sutton. It's a fact.'

'Bollocks,' I said. 'I've seen it with the evidence of my own eyes, FACT.'

'Well, on these numerous occasions you must have seen something else.'

'Seen it, heard it, and smelled it. So have other people from round here.'

At this, Boho started to sob even louder.

Ms Cash handed Boho a tissue. 'I can easily convince Mr Stubbs there are no big monkeys in Sutton.'

'No you can't,' I said.

'No, you can't,' Boho said.

'We are running out of time here,' said Ms Cash. 'Maybe we can schedule another—'

'It's real,' I said. 'I can prove it.'

'Oh, you can, can you, Mr Stubbs?'

'Not here, obviously.'

'Ah, I see.'

'Look, why don't we meet up later in the week. I can show you some things, then we can get these kids to lay off Kyrylo.'

'All right, Mr Stubbs. Why not? I am all for getting everyone to lay off Kyrylo before he or anyone else gets disciplined because of this silly business. But bring me something real to talk about, and in a well-lit public place. Put something on the table. Show me what you've got.'

Boho rocketed up and threw her arms around Ms Cash and they had this big love-in across the desk. A sweet, flowery perfume wafted across me. It must have been hanging off one of them all through the meeting. I didn't like the way I'd only picked up on it now, as if I'd just been frogmarched into another room while somehow staying in my seat.

> • <

All splished and splashed, wearing my newest camouflage-patterned T-shirt and smartest red bandana, I arrived at The Churn, where I'd agreed to meet Ms Cash. I'd tucked a nice big padded envelope under my arm. The blokes by the dartboard – that Paul Pratt with the sovereign rings, that Mobby or Moppy or whatever he's called, the panel beater with the face as moist-looking as crabmeat, and that Tomsky the Tit the State of Florida won't allow back in – they all stopped tossing their arrows and gave it their full 'Monkey magic, monkey magic' chant, followed by some bone-juddering, 'ooooh, oooh, ooooh, you're shit ahhhhs'.

This was what The Funnel calls a 'ritual' that the spanners 'enact' when a 'shaman' (aka Knower) arrives on their turf. It's like: we know you're there, you know we're here, don't come over here, and we won't come over there. According to The Funnel, the same thing happens in the Congo among the Kempanga people when they sense Mokele-Mbembe on their patch. I don't know if this is true, but I don't give the spanners a pass if it's a 'ritual': they'd be making exactly the same sound if they were kicking someone to death outside a Harvester.

Agent MonkeyMagic had been the team name Gorgo gave me during the GIT Supreme days, the years of thunder after Jackie Hogg left and it was me and Gorgo and The Funnel. Yeah: the old days. We'd get the call – *bish*: sighting of ape-like biped; *bosh*, we'd be off in the Abominable Snowmobile, the Geoff Love Orchestra's 'Theme from King Kong' booming out from the cassette deck, off to interrogate new converts or stake out a smallholding somewhere in the dreaming Avalon west of Coulsden. We'd always used codenames in the Reports back then, especially after the Internet went massive and we put the Reports online.

It was a constant aggravation to me that my secret identity had somehow leaked, that the spanners from the Churn had found out that Kevin Stubbs and Agent MonkeyMagic were one and the same. One of these spanners had no doubt told one of his kids about me being Agent MonkeyMagic, and that kid had had the temerity to have a go at my boy. That's why I was here. That's what I was going to sort out, categorically.

I ignored the spanners and pulled up a stool at the bar. I glanced at the framed photos of old, rural, 1900s Sutton arranged around the walls of the public bar: farmland tracks, clapperboard buildings, The Cock when it was still a hotel. These images end at a picture of Bobby Moore lofting the World Cup, as if time stopped there, as if time only ran between 1066 and 1966.

My old mum's house, or the Church of the Poisoned Mind as I sometimes thought of it, was two streets away from here, on Thicket Road. That's where I grew up. That's where Boho and Kyrylo still live, actually. I only left Thicket Road when Boho chucked me out. It was a lot less of a grey house after Boho moved in. She did insist on decorating rather cheerfully, turning that pebble-dashed mausoleum into a garish multicoloured playschool that wasn't really me. When I was growing up there with Mum, smug in her fear of God, smug in her dislikes and her unadventurousness, everything inside and outside was grey. She was grey. The house was grey. The estate was grey. Sutton was grey. Life was grey. Her believing a lot of old shit meant I was kept away from other people, other kids, broader experiences, braver ways of living. I hardly knew any kids who were not scaredy-cat Witness kids. I only saw real, lit-up life in flashes and glimpses, the odd times I was allowed to have tea round someone else's house whose parents were not cranking for Jesus, who didn't see life through a backwards-looking sphincter-sized slit-window of fear, who might let me watch *Tarzan, Lord of the Jungle* or *Arthur C. Clarke's Mysterious World* for five minutes before I was packed off home to her, and her saying no all the time, her saying God will burn me to death in the end. This is why I am a Cell of One, and I really only know Derek Funnel. Derek Funnel reckons that David Lynch was once slated to make a movie in Sutton called *Grey Velvet*. I hope he was joking. I also hope it's true. If enough people say it's true, it will eventually become true, even if David Lynch comes out and say he's never heard of the place.

Anyway: The Greyness. I was round this other kid's house once and he had this Marillion LP, and the colours on the sleeve were so beautiful I almost cried. They were shocking to me. Most of the time when I went out with Mum it was within this gulag archipelago of Witnesses events and houses, all heavily grey; but if we ever went out in Sutton, to the shops, to the supermarket, I could feel some astounding other colour following me: the Red Darkness. Something in Sutton wanted me dead. If I'd told her about it, she would have said it was from Hell, just like if I'd told her about seeing Patty the Patterson-Gimlin Bigfoot on *Arthur C. Clarke's Mysterious World: The Missing Apes* – I'd have had to say seeing it was an accident and they'd made me watch it, just like I'd had to say they made me drink Coca-Cola – she would have said it was a demon, or, if she were in a more frivolous mood, a bloke in a bear suit playing silly-bollocks. The Red Darkness wasn't from Hell. It was from Sutton. It was around every corner. It was in the grey concrete stairwell of the multistorey car park. It glowed behind the trees in Manor Park. It sat behind me at school. It followed me up Thicket Road all the way home. It breathed my name in a dead language. It wanted me.

The day I felt it most powerfully was the day Mum died. She had cancer, breast. She did nothing about it, despite what I begged her to do. I was seventeen by then and at North East Surrey College of Technology taking a BTEC in Computing (and under her radar catching up on all the things I'd missed out on, like Marillion, *Doctor Who*, *Judge Dredd*, and girls, sort of). On the day she died, I was already having a shit time at college – and then on top of that, she died.

I walked all the way home from the hospice in Worcester Park. I felt it closing in, the Red Darkness, trailing me through streets I could hardly see, I was crying so hard. I went into The Churn on my way to Thicket Road.

Technically I was underage, but I always looked big for my age, and always a bit grizzled, like I'd already seen more than I should have seen – even though at that point I'd seen frakk all, really. Might have looked a bit hard as well, as I was wearing my army surplus camouflage jacket. I got served easily. I drank four pints of the lager of Lamot and two nips of Famous Grouse and cried hunched over the bar. No one said anything. No one came over. Young kid in bits. They just gave me a wide berth.

Then whoever they were jumped me on my way out. I don't know how many there were – four at least. They were Chelsea. They had lions on their beany hats. When I regained consciousness I was in hospital. The doctor said I'd suffered a bad head injury. Looked like the left side of my skull had been whacked with a bicycle chain. They let me out a day later. Back in the grey house on Thicket Road, I made some oven chips I couldn't stomach, and on the TV news I saw for the first time the Gartree-Hogg Film, on the news, in my neck of the woods, a Bigfoot: Giganto. Lit up. It was like Arthur C. Dad was trying to tell me something. The Red Darkness was pushed right back into the shadows.

Any one or all of them could have been the guys who jumped me outside this pub: Paul Pratt, Mobby or Moppy or whatever he's called, or Tomsky the Tit.

I tried not to brood on that day, the Day of the Red Darkness. Instead, I tried to imagine all the great things that were going to happen to me when we proved Giganto was real, including getting my family back. I had a pint on the go and a nice big padded envelope I'd placed on the bar, and was mentally patting myself on the back for choosing this craphouse as a meeting place.

Ms Cash wouldn't have the conkers to come in here. She wouldn't turn up.

> • <

She turned up. The place felt too warm all of a sudden. I found myself clawing at the surface of the padded envelope for no good reason.

'You've not seen a ghost as well?' she said.

'I know a man who has,' I said. 'Drink, for your trouble?'

'Sea Breeze, please.'

I ordered her a half of Becks to save her blushes. She didn't complain and perched herself on the barstool next to mine. The spanners from The Churn started to chant, 'Oooh, oooh, oooh, Monkey's on the pull.'

'A pub with a civilised clientele, I see,' she said.

'Nah, this lot are barbaric. It's coming to them one day, you mark my words. When it all kicks off round here, I'll be the one with a sword strapped to his back and an Uzi in each hand, outnumbered a hundred to one but big and strong like I'm on the cover of a *Conan the Barbarian* book, or even the film poster; and then, when I'm out of ammo, I'll free my sword, the Blood-Prow.'

'Yikes.'

'Joke, right? One of those things that don't mean anything.'

'I'm sure Mr Freud would have something to say about that.'

'Why'd you come here?'

'You invited me.'

'That's not an answer.'

'Okay. I promised Bohuslava that I can convince you

there is no relict hominid—'

'Rectal what?'

'*Relict*. Something that has survived from an earlier time. Hominid—'

'I know what a hominid is. It's a Jamiroquai tribute band. What makes you the expert?'

'I've been looking at your website – the gits or whatever – and you and your friends have obviously spent a lot of time looking for this... *cryptid*, and I'm sure, on the occasions you describe, you saw something. I believe that *you* believe that you've seen an apeman. But none of it adds up.'

'How do you know? Looks like you never even go outside.'

'Well, I did my Masters in Primate Behaviour. Then I spent six months out in Sumatra contributing to a research project into the phylogenetic signal and how it relates to the behaviour and territoriality of the local orang-utan population with a view to ensuring their permanent survival.'

'You see the orang pendek out there?'

'He's a myth.'

'That just about sums it all up. I come from Sutton, and I work in IT. So I'd kill to have an opportunity like that, to get out there in the jungle and really test the kit. People like you, you just read the script you're given and it all gets ticked off, box by box. Everyone is kept in their place, the world is kept small and boring and sad and all the great things go unrecognised when they're loping about in the corner of your eye all the time. All you've got to do is believe the evidence of your own eyes, not so-called science.'

'Science is not a script, Kevin. It's a method. All I can say is, okay, there is a remote possibility that in Sumatra, a relict hominid like the hypothetical orang pendek could survive unobserved, because of the ecology equation and the terrain. There are great swathes of unexplored jungle – but here, Kevin, in Sutton, in a built-up area where there's no habitat and no history of large primate populations, no way.'

'How come I've got a freezer full of its scat, then?'

'I'll wager, Kevin, that inside that envelope are a load of grainy, blotchy, pixelated photographs of some splodge in the trees that's a rambler out of focus if it's not a tree stump or – my favourite – an optical illusion. If it's not a man out of focus, it's possibly a man in a monkey suit, if anyone would go to the trouble of messing around like that here. Or, perhaps there may be some pictures of prints in the mud that could be regular human footprints distorted by rain; or at worst, some wag has strapped some plywood cut-outs to his shoes to fool the likes of you and me. What have you got in the envelope? Astonish me.'

As soon as she'd turned up at The Churn I knew I'd made a tactical error. Back at Knower's Ark I'd assembled a choice selection of Giganto evidence: the set of footprints Gorgo and I had taken over at Beddington Sewage Works; stills from the Gartree Hogg/Sutton Cock footage; shots of shredded-up deer we'd found in the Happy Valley. I'd known then that she wasn't going to turn up. She wouldn't have the balls to meet me in The Churn. I would have asked her to meet me in The Dog in Carshalton if I'd actually wanted her to turn up.

So I'd left all my Category Bs on my dining room table, but I took the envelope with me. I don't know why. Maybe I wanted to look formal and aloof in The Churn, on official business, involved in espionage. Maybe I felt reassured by it. When I was a kid I used to have a little bear I carried about to make me feel relaxed. I'd needed to be strong and hard to get over Mum chucking him in the bin because I didn't read all the bits of The Bible I'd promised I would. This was when I was still small, before I was a Knower.

'Look, you've got the wrong end of the stick,' I said. 'Fact of the matter is, I thought you would blow me out.'

'Blow you out? This is not a date, Mr Stubbs.' She plucked the envelope from where I'd re-tucked it under my arm. She squeezed its sides so its seam opened like a mouth. 'Ah, I see. There's nothing in here at all, is there, Kevin? Nothing in the bag. Are you familiar with the term *pareidolia*?'

I didn't say 'yes'. I said, 'Paddy Doyle? Never heard of him.'

'*Pareidolia*. It's when the mind constructs familiar images from random patterns, like when you see a face in tree bark or a plate of bacon and eggs, or Jesus in a muffin.'

'I'm not stupid. If I see a doughnut that looks like Phil Collins's head, I don't think it's going jump up and start singing "Sussudio", do I?'

'People often see what they want to see, and they can take negation as an opportunity not to rethink, but to commit more of themselves to the outcome – the vision, the prophecy, whatever. It happens in cults and millenarian societies.'

'Look. You've not been out there, all night in the woods, waiting, tracking, scanning, using the kit, attracting it, calling, knocking, standing still for ages, blending in with the trees and the grasses. You've not seen it, smelled it, heard it, collected its scat. You're not soaked in The Lore and the Canonicals of it. You've not experienced that thrill when suddenly, for a moment, you glimpse it between the trees – gigantic, proud, alive, part of us, the missing bit of us – and then you admire it, revel in it, how smart it is to leave no traces, how wonderful, majestic, shrewd, clever, undetectable, out there in the woods all alone and unbreakable. You ever feel like that? Unbreakable? Still getting away with it? Not playing by the soppy rulebook – a hero, like the last man who actually came before man?'

Her dippy glasses slid down her nose. For the first time, she seemed to be actually thinking about what I'd been saying.

'Kevin, this all seems rather... don't get me wrong. I'm not disbelieving you, and I'm saying this out of concern, not criticism, but this all seems rather... *tragic* to me. You've got a lovely son who you've driven away. You're separated from your lovely wife. You're running around in the woods, chasing shadows, probably wasting all your money, and squandering your opportunities, too. If you want to rebuild your relationship with Kyrylo, you need to drop all this childish whimsy. And call it women's intuition—'

'That's not scientific, is it?'

'No, it's not, but Bohuslava still has a lot of affection for you. I can tell. She just doesn't want to be married to a man who prioritises a... yeti, something that doesn't exist, over family life. She cares for you. That's why she's asked me to do this, and in psychological terms this fixation of yours seems emblematic of a juvenile desire to escape the responsibilities of adulthood, marriage and child-rearing...'

Her eyes were like gleaming blue pebbles. Her voice was quite nice sounding if you only listened to the musical sounds she was making, and turned your brain off. I could have fallen asleep if she'd kept it up.

'Mr Stubbs?' she said. 'You all right? Did anything I said register?'

'It's real,' I said. 'I've seen it – and yes, I would kill to see my son again, yes, I would, but it's real. Even if I lie and say it's not real for a quiet life, it'll still be real, it'll still be out there. So, the way I look at it is this: if I get the evidence, it's real; and if it's real, Boho and me will be fine and my boy will come back to me. More than that, he'll get it now and think I'm a hero, the hero-dad who solved it all.'

'It's not real, Kevin.'

'It is.'

'Then there's only one thing for it. I'm going to have to join your team.'

'You? Don't make me laugh.'

'I've trekked in rougher places than this.'

'Look, if it were up to me, I'd love to have you ride shotgun, but it's not. It's not my call. Here.'

I held my hands up. This is where I brought it all on myself. I thumbed through my wallet until I found it. I gave her Gorgo's card.

She looked over it, chewing her bottom lip like she was solving a Sudoku, and then she said, all whispery, husky: 'Gigantopithecus Intelligence Team.'

Whatever happened next was an accident.

FACT: We banged heads.

FACT: I wasn't trying to snog her.

FACT: It was totally out of order of her to say that the accidental banging of heads proved to her that 'malecrisis-mountainstrongholdism' dominated my 'psychological outlook', that I only see what I want to see – that, in her words, 'You saw I had made myself sexually available to you when I'd only shown an awareness of the traumas you keep secret.'

> • <

A week after my meeting with Maxine at The Churn, Gorgo summoned me. I'd never been invited to his house before. Something big must have happened. If he was only going to tell me that he'd sent Maxine off with a flea in her ear, he would have met me in The Churn, surely.

As he poured me a coffee, he told me that Mrs Gorgo was at a timeshare in Gran Canaria with her sister for ten days. He had the place to himself for once.

'The cat's away,' he said. He handed me a cigar, smiling that million-dollar smile that could have won him an election if he'd chosen a different path in life.

He was looking old, though. Age was eating into his face, had been for years. Crow's feet scratched under his eyes. The grooves of his forehead seemed to be getting deeper.

He was quiet as he pottered around his conservatory, setting up the projector screen and booting up his laptop. His hip cracked when he sauntered to the back of the conservatory to dim the lights. This crack would come for me one day. This is how it goes for the Knowers. This is what it would be like for me if we didn't nail Giganto soon. One day I would wake up merely shadowboxing; my bones would creak and crackle as I looked back unhappily at a life spent waiting in the rain for the Great Confirmation.

I clipped the end of my cigar and sparked up. 'Our esteemed cryptozoologist making an appearance?'

'Nah, my old lady'll chop my bollocks off if she thinks I've let him in the house again,' said Gorgo. 'Remember the last time? And I need to talk to you about something, old son.

But before we discuss anything, I want us to go back to the beginning.'

Rain pattered on the conservatory roof. Outside, rain fell on the tarmac and paving slabs of Sutton. Rain fell on all the forests and smallholdings of north Surrey.

We pulled our chairs in front of the screen. I didn't need to watch the film again. It played in my dreams. I could reconstruct it second by second with my eyes closed. I passed through Sutton Cock all the time, on my lunch break, doing my shopping, and I always felt the film reconstructing itself about me. It was as if I were actually in the film, as if I had been there with the original Men with Kit at the time. Didn't matter if it was day or night. Didn't matter that most of the shops had changed since 1988. I was there all the time anyway, but watching it again tonight, and watching it with Gorgo, that just lit me up, my own private 5th of November.

The first fifteen seconds: loads of blur and smudge and the tubing effect that reflects off the street lights as Gorgo tries to steady the camera, until he gets himself under control and a moving, dark outline clarifies dead centre.

On the other side of the crossroads now, you can clearly see the dark outline hesitate in front of the window of Knobs and Knockers, a shop that sells door handles. The dark outline's back is turned but in the shop's lights it's clearly gigantic, hairy, with long swinging arms and a cone-shaped head. It's a dirty great gigantopithecus, no doubt about it.

Next, it flicks its head, its glowing red eyes clearly visible. This is the moment that messed with Jackie Hogg.

The next bit is the bit that sent great tremors of Revelation through me when I first saw it on TV. The lope. You get the lope as Giganto sways across the road. Arm-swing is clearly visible. He knows now he's being observed. He can sense the eyes of the kit on him, so he picks up speed.

He disappears into the alley that led to Carats nightclub.

The film goes dead.

Even though I have seen this film ten thousand times; even though I can summon it at will, like I have a photographic memory; even though I feel that sometimes I live in that film, that I was actually there when the Originals were making it, I'm still lit up watching it here. It's like I've all over again been promised something here, chosen.

But looking back on that night, this viewing was somehow the best ever, the realest, because it was just me and him at his HQ: me and Gorgo, the Man Who Started It All, the man who gave me the opportunity, the man I owed everything. I would do anything for him. I would go over the top. I would drop out of a plane. I would go into any wood, at the worst hour of any night, follow any scream, any stench, keep going, keep filming when anyone else would have bricked it. Me and Gorgo: we had gone together into the darkness hunting for the light.

He stubbed out his cigar and came straight out with it.

'Kevin, old son. You and me, we've been doing this a long time. A long, long time. And we've had some times. We've come close. You know we've come close. And we're getting closer. Things are afoot, old son. I can feel it in my waters. I can feel it in the air. I've heard whispers out there. People are talking – can't tell you which people, don't want to put you in danger, what with you being a family man and that. But, it's going to happen soon: the Great Confirmation. It's just around the corner. I know I've said that a hundred times over the years, but this time it's for real. Nothing is going to be the same for anyone ever again. Not round here. Not anywhere. And I've been giving this a lot of thought. I'm a busted flush, mate. Don't know if it's the way the cold gets into my bones out there now. But it's time for me to step aside. It's time for Agent Gorgo to give way to the younger generation.'

This couldn't be. He couldn't quit, not after what he'd just said, that the Great Confirmation would soon be here. We needed a leader for that. And then it struck me, what he was actually saying.

Who would now lead the GIT?

Kevin Stubbs: loyal henchman and hardcore Knower, with tons of kit and over twenty years' experience tracking the legendary North Surrey Gigantopithecus shoulder-to-shoulder with legends like Gorgo Gartree and Jackie Hogg?

Or Derek Funnel: works in Waterstone's Sutton?

It was going to be me, surely.

'I know, Kevin – I can see it in your face that you're asking yourself who should lead now. Listen to me, something big is coming. We need to be at our best. I need someone plausible to take it from here, and you and I, we know that can't be Derek. I love Derek like a son, like a weird middle son, but to people who aren't Knowers yet... you know exactly what I'm getting at. So, we need someone plausible, someone who can play the media like a fiddle, and we need someone demure. You have a lot of qualities, Kevin, but you ain't demure, son. Put you in front of a news conference... They won't get it. You're a master of shadows, son, a tracker, man of the woods, a partisan of romance, that sort of thing. You've got to lead from the rear echelon. So, that's why I've decided to give over command to that monkey-puzzle woman you sent my way last week.'

Now, I'd been passed over many times in my life already: at school, at work, and then in my marriage and my parenting. Sometimes I cared, sometimes I didn't. But now I was being passed over in the GIT. The GIT: the only thing that mattered to me. And it was Gorgo who was doing this to me; Gorgo, who had been more like a father to me than anyone, since I never got to meet Arthur C. Clarke – he was passing me over for some Jenny-come-lately who wasn't even a Knower.

'Mate,' he went. 'Don't take this hard. Dry your eyes. And don't you say "chain of command" now, when I know you mean eff you. Listen, mate, we are close to it. We need PR now. We need to be legit. This move may sound shonky, but this move has a name, Kevin, a proper name that you'll love. It's called the Fig Leaf Stratagem, and only you and me are in on the Fig Leaf Stratagem. That's proper GIT, that is. When the Great Confirmation comes, they'll believe her. It'll all be your work, but it will be believed. You want us to be believed, don't you?'

'You're saying we've hired her, right?'

'That's right, Kevin. She's hired, but you ain't fired, son. And listen, don't you let on and get all surly and insubordinate. Do as she says. You might even learn something. She knows her tails from her talons. It's all useful for when he have to talk to those who struggle with this thing of ours.'

Taking a last pull on the stub-end of my cigar, I sucked on the juice in my mouth until it tasted strong and bitter. I had to accept the Fig Leaf Stratagem. I would do my best and try to learn from Maxine to make me a better investigator, but it wasn't going to get as far as Gorgo reckoned. She'd quickly stray out of her depth, quit when she came face-to-face with a dirty great gigantopithecus out in the woods. She wouldn't be able to take the hit to her sanity score when the great twenty-sided die rolled. After we had Category A proof – like, say, a film of something gigantic in the woods she couldn't explain – one of the hardcore Knowers (aka me) would have to assume command, and soon after that we would light up the real world for my boy to see.

That moment had arrived: the Hour of the Beast of Banstead Common.

GIGANTOPITHECUS INTELLIGENCE TEAM

REPORT #214 (CATEGORY A)

SECTION 5

We finally arrived at the witness's residence at approximately 19.00. The witness greeted us with evident suspicion, and throughout the meeting he seemed restless. We were invited into a lounge area where several pre-school children were playing. Shouting and laughing could be heard from upstairs. A woman, seemingly unbothered by our presence, prepared food in a kitchen to the rear of the property.

GIT Cryptozoologist Funnel investigated the rear of the building. GIT Investigator Stubbs and I initially discussed the sighting with the witness in the lounge area. There was a discussion about money.

The witness then reiterated his account of the sighting as filed on 8 July, but it contained discrepancies and inconsistencies. This time, the cryptid was reported as howling as it made its way through the trees, and had smashed a log against surrounding trunks. I made some attempt to discuss these details but the witness rambled and was evasive. When asked to provide names and contact details for the other co-witnesses, the witness became aggressive.

However, GIT was able to obtain a copy of the mobile phone footage of the sighting. It was agreed that the footage would not be distributed.

I cannot consider this witness to be a credible one.

GIT Cryptozoologist Funnel seemed nervous about viewing the footage while the GIT van was still parked outside the witness's residence.

There was some discussion about where to view the footage, and eventually it was agreed that we would view the film at my residence, not in the van or in the Butterchurn public house.

Note: it was at this point that I raised concerns, after I discovered that the so-called 'Banstead Bigfoot' clip had already been posted on YouTube.

REPORT #214:
THE FACTS BY KEVIN STUBBS:
SECTION FIVE

Quite a lot more went on in that house than Sci-Borg mentions in her report, including a dirty great scream that came from nowhere and shook us all to the core.

We were standing in the witness's front room – MonkeyMagic, The Funnel and Sci-Borg – all trembling with excitement (except for Sci-Borg). It was a weirdly empty house. There were no carpets or plants or pictures. The sofa in the front room was so old that if it had a brain, it would probably remember watching *Arthur C. Clarke's Mysterious World*. A plasma TV about the same size as Kent hung from the wall. All these kids were chasing each other around and acting like we were not even there. I smiled and gave this limp wave that I hoped none of the other grown-ups saw. Part of me wanted to join in and chase the little rascals around the sofa pretending to be a Gigantopithecus. Another part wanted to pack up and find my own kid, get through to him in some way. Then I remembered why I was here.

The witness (aka Gavin Brunt) was sprawled on the sofa. He hadn't even got up when we rang the bell. His missus had opened the door, a moody-looking brunette who took one look at us and shouted, 'Get rid, Gav,' over her shoulder before she slouched off.

He was one of those blokes you see a lot in Sutton. Probably still in his thirties, but he looked about sixty, his face pale and dry and creased. I knew the type. I remembered the

Chelsea Lion patches and stud earrings, and the ten seconds it took for me to register that the bike chain had whacked my left temple, and the other ten for me to lose consciousness and hit my head again on the ground and wake up a day later in a white room and she was still dead and I couldn't see straight.

The witness had told Sci-Borg on the phone that he'd once been a DJ at one of those thump-thump nightclubs that over the last twenty years had spread across Sutton like the clap in a Wild West frontier town. His boogie nights ended long ago. One day the room had emptied, the sun had come up, and it was still hurting his eyes. And, yes, he was restless and he fidgeted. This is understandable. He'd seen something that had thrown all his certainties into the meat-grinder. He'd seen a gigantopithecus, rampant. This kicks out the psychological brackets that prop up a personality. People deal with it in different ways. I downed two cans of Stella after I saw my first gigantopithecus.

Sci-Borg clicked her fingers like she was Mary Poppins and commanded all the kids to leave their own front room (she calls herself a school teacher; this took about half an hour, she should have asked me to do it but that is the story of my life). Then she ordered The Funnel off to 'do his thing'. She was always sending him away to take readings in places guaranteed not to give any readings, so afterwards she could say we hadn't found anything.

'So, Mr Brunt,' she said, 'let's see if we can get this sorted out for you.'

'What sorted?'

'We're going to help you decide what exactly it was that you saw on Saturday night.'

'I saw something.'

'I'm sure you did, but it could have been a lot of things, and it was dark, and you were a long way away from it, and in boisterous company. Could we perhaps start by going over your witness statement? What exactly happened on Saturday night?'

'I've already told you twice.'

'I know, but it's important that we're clear about the details.'

'It was like I said. My mate saw it first. It was in the trees, right, this big, hairy thing watching the kids. Then it moves off. Freaky long arms and these killer red eyes. And then, right, it let off this howl, like it were trying to scare us, and it smacked this tree with a branch.'

All my hairs on my arms and my neck were prickling. If I hadn't seen it myself, tons of times, I would have been jealous.

'That's what we call a gigantopithecus,' I told him. 'There's no need to be scared of it. It's pretty gentle, unless you're a deer, or you get between it and a deer, or it and a jar of Sunpat Crunchy.'

'Kevin, please. Look, Mr Brunt, neither in your written statement, nor when we discussed this on the telephone, did you mention either the wood knock or the howl. Why's that?'

This was typical Sci-Borg. Just because The DJ had changed his story, doesn't mean that his account is suspect. In fact, it's perfectly normal to finesse the statement after the event. I've done it loads of times. In 'The Case of the Nonsuch Park Kong' (Report #031) it was only *afterwards* that I realised I'd seen the gigantopithecus emerge from the trees to scoop water from a puddle. At the time I thought I'd only seen an indistinct but large shape somewhere in the trees. It wasn't surprising that The DJ remembered more about the sighting a couple of days later. This is just how the mind works.

'Well, there's only one thing for it,' said Sci-Borg. 'Can you please allow us to copy the camera film? We'll study it and report back to you in complete confidence.'

The DJ went, quite coolly, I reckoned, 'Dawkers says it's worth six grand. Min.'

'Mr Stubbs, will you fetch Mr Funnel,' said Sci-Borg. 'We're leaving.'

I wasn't going to let her ruin this for me, not when I could sense it shimmering and reaching out to me, all Holy Grail, and stored on the mobile phone I could see peeping out from the pocket of The DJ's hoodie.

I stepped forward, manned up. I put my hand across Sci-Borg's front and stared into The DJ's soul.

'Look, mate. I know what you saw. You know what you saw. I have been waiting for this moment for all my life. So, give it to me. Now.'

He takes his phone out of his pocket, prods at it, and hands it over to me – not Sci-Borg. This just emphasises the importance of local knowledge and winning over hearts and minds. I then went about the highly skilled IT-guy work of emailing the file to Sci-Borg's laptop. Meanwhile, she asked him, 'These other people you were with on Saturday, do you have names, addresses and phone numbers?'

A dirty great scream came from the rear of the house.

I looked at Sci-Borg and she looked at me. The Funnel burst through a door. I half-expected to see Giganto looming behind him, about to rip him to shreds like a deer or devour him like a bagel slathered with Sunpat Crunchy, but he was being chased by Summer, The DJ's other half, slapping him over the head with a pizza box.

> • <

This was all a misunderstanding, of course, though it has to be said that The Funnel collects misunderstandings like I collect scat samples.

This is what he told me and Sci-Borg back in the van afterwards. I am not saying I believe this, as I saw none of it with the evidence of my own eyes. I'm just reporting what he told us. However, he is a genius, and geniuses tend to be right.

He'd found himself in this little stone-slab garden round the back of The DJ's house. There was a wooden bird table out there, but the pole had been snapped in two. That pole was about six inches thick, thus hard to break: this is what we call a clear, one-hundred-per-cent Category B gigantopithecus sighting. You'd have to be a gigantopithecus to break something that sturdy.

The Funnel thinks the gigantopithecus disturbs the Earth's magnetic field, so he took out his electromagnetic field reader (aka The Tractor Beam).

He startled at once. The readings were off the hook. The Trifield was going mental, and went even more mental as The Funnel stepped closer to the house. It went absolutely berserk when he reached the kitchen door.

What he experienced then, as he stepped into the kitchen, was an out-of-phase time-slip experience so strong he could only compare it to the ones he'd had in Tibet. A tunnel of yellow light whirred around him. For a second he thought he was actually his pen name, Tom Egatherion, and it was 1913 and he has writing a book called *The Book of Lies* and he was having it off with an actual woman in a room full of candles with chalk marks on the floor, and all these blokes in KKK-style hoods were standing about watching and singing some sort of hymn; he'd been in the tunnel of whirring yellow light forever. Weird music was playing. It was like he was stuck in an early Genesis LP, or the track by that Marillion, 'Grendel', the one that bollocks on for so long that you want to top yourself, but it had been playing over and over and over again and it was driving the whole world suicidal. He saw our soldiers rush over the top of the trenches and Hitler shouting and the atom bomb going off and the Yanks napalming the jungle and the Bluff Creek Bigfoot turn its head and lope back into the woods, imperiously, and the North Surrey Gigantopithecus lope into the dark at Sutton Cock, imperiously, and then he saw an imperious bald bloke being dragged out of a pile of bloody fur that he assumed was him being reborn in the future again as Tom Egatherion.

At the end of the whirring yellow tunnel he could see a shape, and as he stepped towards the shape he could see a pyramid, and at the heart of that pyramid was an eye. He found himself chanting: *novus ordo seclorum, novus ordo seclorum*, 'a new order for the ages', the catchphrase of the Illuminati. He could see the All-Seeing Eye at the heart of the pyramid. He could see the Serpent's Eye.

He knew from all his reading, and from all the bammers and nutjobs he'd met in Asia, that the gigantopithecus had appeared because The DJ and Summer must be the reincarnation of Adam and Eve. When the Serpent (aka the gigantopithecus) promises Adam and Eve that their eyes will be opened if they eat the fruit of the Tree of Good and Evil (aka have a barbecue in a Giganto hotspot), that eye is the eye of the mind and means KNOWING, that eye is also the Eye of Osiris and the All-Seeing Eye of the Freemasons. One of The DJ's and/or Summer's kids is called Mason.

This is what he told us, anyway. Contrary to what he says, though, a gigantopithecus is clearly an animal, a better version of us, not a time-travelling ghost-thing from another world.

> • <

According to Summer – who told The DJ, who later told us – she was cooking a pizza in the microwave, and when the oven pinged, this weird crackle she'd noticed but hadn't reacted to or investigated because she is generally a moody sort, stopped. I reckon this must have been the Trifield 100XE shutting down. She then felt something prodding the small of her back. She turned to find The Funnel stroking the tattoo of the Cuban rapper Pitbull's face that was winking out from the strip of uncovered skin above the waistline of her trackie bottoms. That's when she attacked him with the pizza box and drove him into the front room.

> • <

Quick as a flash, my right hand was around The DJ's throat to keep him from decking The Funnel. Meanwhile, Sci-Borg was inspecting Summer's back.

'Keep still. No, no, there's no mystical symbol here.'

'He's an angel,' said The Funnel. 'She's married to an angel. They have practised sex magick, in this very house.'

By now I had The DJ's file on my phone. I had The DJ in one hand, my body wedged between his, scrabbling and kicking, and The Funnel backing himself into the TV. In my eye line, I've got Sci-Borg conducting rigorous scientific investigations down some moody sort's tracksuit.

'They know us,' shouted The Funnel. 'They're coming.'

I assumed command. I knew I was going to have to at some point tonight. I'd expected it would be after we'd seen the film, and the Great Confirmation reduced Sci-Borg to a puddle of sludge. This was even earlier than I'd hoped.

'Shut it, you drokker, get in the van. And Lead Investigator, leave her arse alone. We've got what we came for. Run.'

The moment we got into the van – the moment I knew that the footage was ours – was the best moment of my life so far. Not only did we have the film that, as far as I was concerned, had a one hundred per cent chance of bringing about the Great Confirmation, I had stepped up in there and got it for us, and I'd got one over on one of the Sutton Lot. I was the hero. I was finally winning. I was leading, showing the team the way.

> • <

I wouldn't usually let Sci-Borg drive the Abominable. That night, though, because I'd had to get the women and children out first and provide covering fire, she had taken the driver's seat. The Funnel was shotgun, shaking with nerves. He was fingering this clown amulet thing I'd never seen before, like it was comforting him in some way. While he babbled about what had really happened between him and Summer, and Hitler, and Marillion and *The Book of Lies*, I was in the back having a good old muck about with my phone. As we raced away with our precious cargo of gigantopithecus evidence, Sci-Borg was giving The Funnel this lecture about 'snatching at straws'.

'That man is unreliable,' she said, 'we can't possibly believe a word he says.'

Sci-Borg basically thinks that your opinion can only be trusted if you come from a certain background. If on 6 July, the gigantopithecus had appeared further south on Banstead Commons, towards the nice bit of Surrey, where the nice people live, hers would have been a completely different story. If they'd had a gazebo up and there was a knob playing a gramophone or pricks standing about in stripy blazers and straw hats all singing at once or playing ukuleles, and if it was Dr Rupert Oilly Prat entertaining friends with quails' eggs and croissants, and they'd got a bit squiffy on the champers, then experienced the feeling of being watched and smelled the horrible smell and saw it standing there in the trees, with its cone-shaped head rampant and long arm raised, then Sci-Borg would have gone: Category A sighting, I have solved the mystery of the North Surrey Gigantopithecus. Just because The DJ isn't posh doesn't mean he didn't see a gigantopithecus.

'All those nutters and psychos The DJ hangs about with,' I said, 'who saw Giganto on Saturday – they'll be in The Churn now. We need to head over there. One of them runs the Chicago Rock.'

'There's no need,' she said, 'we've got the film.'

'Jesus' tits. Half the Sutton lot saw it, and they'll be in there.'

'*Say* they saw it. *Say*, Kevin. It doesn't mean anything.'

'They saw it because it wanted them to see it,' said The Funnel. He was holding up the clown amulet thing to the windscreen like a strip of film before a light box.

'I've had enough of you today, Mr Funnel,' said Sci-Borg. 'I want you two to look at this no doubt ridiculous film. We'll get this crossed off once and for all.'

'It knows,' said The Funnel. 'It knows you doubt it. It can sense such vibrations. It will prove itself to you.'

'You can come to mine, I'll make us some omelettes.'

Job done. I had no intention of hitting The Churn. I'd just needed to throw a little dust in the Sci-Borg's CCTV camera of a head before we got to analyse the footage.

> • <

Back at Sci-Borg's flat, the first thing she did was tell us to stay in the kitchen-diner. Then she went around the place closing all the doors and asked us nicely not to go in any of the other rooms. To be honest, I think she meant The Funnel, rather than me.

While she was away, Oedipuss (aka her cat) went mental. It sprang at The Funnel and tried to eviscerate his wedding tackle. I took the little scamp and eased it onto next-door's balcony, where it duly started to force itself on a mini-conifer. I'm talking about the cat here, not The Funnel.

The Funnel joined me on the balcony.

'I don't know about you,' he said, 'but this night has reminded me not just that I have climbed mountaintops before, but that I will climb mountains again.'

'Nah, it's the trees I keep seeing. I see the trees in my dreams.'

We looked out over the dreaming lights of Sutton, the hills a soft, dark swell in the distance.

'Let your dreams ripple through you, Stubbs,' said The Funnel, 'remind you that once this was Andreasweald, the most ancient of English forests. This was the home of the Long Men until the Normans came and hunted them for sport, driving them into the caves and crevasses.'

I found myself filling up with tears at this thought: the noble and pure gigantopithei being driven into the dark, only to appear once in a blue moon to reveal themselves to the Knowers or to rip a deer to shreds or shit-up a camper.

We had the gigantopithecus on film now. I'd never felt so excited, so on the brink of something great. I'd read about some American with a massive bouff worse than The Funnel's, who said that you have to put in ten thousand hours to become great.

No doubt about it, I had put in my ten thousand hours. I had put in ten thousand hours of tracking and calling and banging trees with sticks and camping out and collecting hair and scat and making plaster casts of footprints and recording howls in the night and seeing the thing with the evidence of my own eyes, seeing it peep from behind trees, run across fields, disappear into the loving blackness of the night and the woods.

At that moment, on the balcony, mesmerised and staring into the red winking lights and what remained of Andreasweald, The Funnel and I were truly standing on the shoulders of Giganto. It should have been my boy with me, of course. That was the only thing that would have made the moment sweeter.

I wasn't going to let Sci-Borg bollocks this up. I'd taken a precautionary measure. She came back into the kitchen-diner. She'd changed out of her field-trip costume. She started to prance about the kitchen, cracking eggs and chopping herbs (I hate herbs, but I didn't say anything), so I booted up the laptop and connected to the web – and *banzai*, it was there, whipping up a viral storm already.

'Drokk it,' I said as loudly as I could, then kicked Sci-Borg's bin.

'Whatever is the matter?' she said, turning to me with a frying pan in her hand that she probably calls a skillet.

'The footage,' I said. 'Some drokker has already posted it online.'

'How on earth did that happen?'

'Told you. Can't trust those spanners from the estate.'

I have to admit that I had been a bit snide. I'd stitched The DJ right up. He'd take the flack for this. When I'd emailed the file to Sci-Borg Max, I'd bcc'd myself in, and while we were in the back of the Abominable I'd uploaded the footage to Dark Static TV, one of my many YouTube aliases.

Sci-Borg put the skillet down on the hob and came over to the laptop.

'Oh dear. I was hoping this wouldn't make us look stupid for once.'

The film had already attracted a thread of comments. Right at the top, straight in, was a posting from someone calling himself Fortean Tony:

```
Oh dear. Typically, the camerawork is uneven.
Typically, the subject is blotchy. Typically,
you can't really see very much at all. But
```

```
even so, the shin rise and the arm swing
are incompatible with that of a great ape.
Verdict: man in a suit.
```

And then a user called Man_in_a_Suit claimed it was him in a suit trying to audition for a proper British horror film with Danny Dyer and Craig Fairbrass already slated to star. Someone calling herself Sos_the_Rope said it was 'MonkeyMagic' (aka me) 'acting the giddy goat'. There was a lot of snide sneering at the children's clothes and the 'poor diction' of The DJ's mates (we didn't all go to Eton or Rampton). Then some knob called BeezerGeezer comes in with:

```
No one's going to believe this until we have
a body. Why didn't they just go up and lamp
it? Take a bat to it? Shoot it, then drive it
around Sutton on a forklift so we can all see
it? This shit needs to be dealt with once and
for all.
```

Someone called NatterJaqui got the right hump with BeezerGeezer:

```
Have any of these people who are posting
things like 'take a bat to it', 'lamp it',
'shoot it' ever thought that he might want to
be left alone in peace??? He's probably just
a new primate. How would you like it if you
were constantly getting chased, filmed and
put on the Internet? OK, you would probably
feel nice because of the popularity, but
```

he doesn't deserve to get shot or put on
a forklift. Just think about what you are
saying, you animals. You should be shot. You
should be put in a zoo.

'She's got a point,' I said, trying to act like I was all Zen
samurai, cold and analytical, when what I really fancied
doing was giving Sci-Borg's bin another kick-in, release
some of the adrenaline that was scalextricking around my
veins.

'Let's not get distracted by this,' said Sci-Borg. 'We ought
to watch it ourselves before either of you is tempted to
respond.'

Omelette was served. The three of us sat at her kitchen bar
to dissect what was already known internationally as The
Banstead Bigfoot Film.

GIGANTOPITHECUS INTELLIGENCE TEAM

REPORT #214 (CATEGORY A)

SECTION 6

<u>Analysis: 'The Banstead Bigfoot' footage</u>

The first forty-five seconds of the footage corresponds roughly to the eyewitness account. A small girl is looking up at the camera, arms held across her chest and wiggling her hips to the beat of the very loud dance music playing in the background. A voice, presumably that of co-witness Mr Dawkers, draws the attention of the witness to someone standing in the nearby trees. Mr Dawkers attributes a possible motive to the subject. The camera remains pointed at the grass while shouting erupts off-shot.

At this point, the camera is raised. The treeline is out of focus. Light quality is generally poor. A large figure is discernible at the top right of the frame. The figure is not clearly visible, though it would appear to be man-sized. It is not clear, due to the distance, camera jerks, intervention of foliage and the poor light, but there could be something on the subject's back. The arms do appear to be extended and swing when the subject strides across the frame. Halfway across the frame, the subject does appear to turn towards the camera as it crosses a gap in the treeline. Its eyes appear to be red. The trees then obscure it. The camera is switched off. The 'sighting' section of the footage lasts 5.3 seconds.

> • <

It is typical of such sightings that the light is poor, the footage unstable and the images indistinct. Pausing the film and zooming in causes the subject to pixilate beyond recognition. In such cases, the subject could be many other things besides a gigantopithecus.

The 'Banstead Bigfoot' is most visible at the moment it appears to glance back as it crosses a gap in the trees. Here it runs with short strides, with the rear leg knee-locked and with hoiked-up elbow movements. Contrary to the account supplied by the witness, the subject appears to move rather ponderously and without the urgency associated with a shy and frightened animal. This does not correspond with large primate locomotion and would suggest that the subject is human.

The eyes that glint at this point in the footage do so too brightly and neatly and would appear to have more in common with dashboard warning lights than the 'eye shine' associated with animals at night.

There is some audio but the general commotion that accompanies the footage obscures any possible vocalisations coming from the subject.

Here is a transcript of some of the audio:

[female screaming]
'…paedo, paeeeeeeeedo… paeeeeeeeedo…'

There is no conclusive evidence that the witnesses did see a gigantopithecus on 6 July. The subject of the film could easily be a heavy-set golfer carrying a bag and clubs towards the nearby golf course. Or this could easily be another deliberate hoax.

However, there was some disagreement within GIT as to the conclusiveness of this analysis. It was eventually agreed that the team would investigate the area of the sighting at the next convenient juncture.

REPORT #214:
THE FACTS BY KEVIN STUBBS:
SECTION SIX

'The "sighting" section of the footage lasts 5.3 seconds.' Sci-Borg implies in Report #214 that this is a problem, as if what comes before the appearance of the gigantopithecus isn't part of the sighting. The Funnel did try to set her straight.

'The footage that precedes the appearance of the Long Man, where nymphs enact a dance of beckoning and the men shout words of warning, is a ritual in which the Long Man is invited, then barred from participation in human society. This ritual is similar in form to the M'Prith ritual of the Kempanga pygmy tribe of northern Congo. There, Mokele-Mbembe is first enticed by a complicated system of hand flicks, dance steps and hip shimmies by topless nymphs, before the virile men of the tribe, the true hunters, loft spears and machetes to show what will happen to it if it intrudes on their territory.'

'Shush, Derek. I'm concentrating.'

'The ritual recapitulates a ceremony of human–gigantopithecus diplomacy that has gone on subconsciously for thousands of years, and is repeated in all areas of the world where apemen have been sighted.'

'Pure conjecture, or quite possibly made-up nonsense.'

I didn't get involved in any of this. I sat it out. I wasn't going to say anything. I'd wait until we moved on to what we were going to do to further the investigation. Sitting in Sci-Borg's kitchen with a real live gigantopithecus caught on camera before me, I knew that I had it. The first documented footage of the North Surrey Gigantopithecus since Gartree-Hogg/ Sutton Cock in 1988. Science was going to get rebooted once this ran front-page in the *Daily Mail*.

'Derek, look at it,' said Sci-Borg. 'What you see there could be many other things besides a gigantopithecus.'

'You're not taking into account, Lead Investigator, that its gift is deception.'

'Animals don't deceive. Not in the sense you mean, anyway.'

'Its magic is in causing change to occur in conformity with its will.'

'Let me repeat myself, Derek: what we see there could be something else besides a gigantopithecus, if—'

The Funnel gave me a nod. He needed my help.

'Just because it *could* be many other things besides a gigantopithecus,' I said, 'doesn't means it isn't.'

'Kevin, it's extinct. So, what you see on that film is more likely to be a—'

'Yeah, yeah. Gartree-Hogg was a pantomime cat. The Nonsuch Kong was a heron on a bollard. The Hackbridge Howl was two foxes having it off. Listen, you can't confuse a gigantopithecus with a cat, or a heron. You can't confuse a gigantopithecus with two foxes having it off. You can't confuse a gigantopithecus with a former British heavyweight boxer leaving a nightclub. You can't confuse a gigantopithecus with a dozen grey squirrels going mental in a tree. And for the last time, you can't confuse a gigantopithecus with a man in a monkey suit. We don't walk right. Our arms and legs are not the same length. They have massive feet and a cone-shaped head. It can't be done.'

'Look at this footage, Kevin. It's all unstable and indistinct.'

'Have you ever tried to film a gigantopithecus on the move? It's not that easy. Gorgo was a trained cameraman, and even he couldn't keep the lens still at Sutton Cock. Our witnesses are almost never well prepared. The horrible smell gets to them. They get shat up. The DJ's hardly a top wildlife cameraman, and he was ripped to his tits on booze. You can't expect to have a nice, neat, crystal-clear shot of the thing.'

'Who do you want to take us seriously? Him—' She flicked her thumb sideways at The Funnel. '—or *National Geographic*?'

'It's no coincidence,' said The Funnel, 'that all films of the Long Man are, as you say, unstable and indistinct – not because of any fear it instils in the unprepared viewer, but because alien technology and cloaking devices cause electrical equipment to go on the fritz. They *want* us to see them this way.'

'I forgot it's an alien now,' said Sci-Borg. 'One ET standing on another ET wrapped in a fur coat. I can't really put that in the report. It's utter—'

'It's staring you in the face,' I said, 'but you'd still rather believe it's an owl seen from a funny angle, or some fish and chips left out in the rain, or the Hominid Rex logo sprayed on a fence, or—'

'Kevin, do you want to see your son again?'

'This is it. The Great Confirmation. He sees this, he'll Know. He'll get it. He'll want to come out with me. He'll want to see it.'

'I don't see it, I don't see it, I don't see it. I look at this film and I don't see anything that will convince anyone besides you two.'

'There is only one thing for it,' said The Funnel, still fiddling with his new clown necklace thing. 'We must reconvene tomorrow to inspect the site.'

'I'll bring the kit,' I said.

'I strongly disagree,' said Sci-Borg. 'There's nothing on this tape that suggests there's any reason to go out there.'

'Nothing?' I said. 'There's a dirty great gigantopithecus—'

'And I don't think it's a good idea that we turn up at that man's house again.'

'You can't pick your witnesses,' I said. 'You don't believe anyone unless they're some Gwapplemegwapenuts Mr Spock type—'

'What is the point of me being Lead Investigator if you're both going to ignore me? You both have better things to be doing with your lives than this, surely?'

'I think, then,' said The Funnel, 'that the best thing to do is for Mr Stubbs and myself to take things from here. We're rarely alerted to a sighting so soon afterwards. People are usually reluctant to come forward. It may still be in the area. It may well come back. I suggest we collect the witness at six tomorrow.'

'Okay, okay, okay,' said Sci-Borg. 'But I do not want you two going round there unsupervised. All hell will break loose. I will contact Mr Brunt. Kevin, bring the van here after work tomorrow. We'll take Mr Brunt back to the Common. You...' She pointed at The Funnel, quite aggressively, actually. '... meet us at the site. And I want this settled once and for all. There is no apeman in Sutton.'

She turned her back and took out a half-full bottle of pink wine from her fridge. I realised that I'd left my phone on the balcony. I went out to get it. When I came back, as if by magic The Funnel had vanished.

Sci-Borg was standing there, all willowy and barefoot with a wine glass pressed to her lips and giving me this weird stare. There was nothing too bad about the stare in itself (I've had far worse stares from women) but I realised this must be the first time I'd been alone with a woman (at least not in a public place like The Churn or The Dog, not outdoors, not at work, not in some agreed neutral space with Boho) for a long time. Even though I have stood in the trees for ten thousand hours eyeball-to-eyeball with giant-sized gigantopithei, cold fear came over me.

'Kevin, can we talk?' she said. 'Let's go out onto the balcony.'

She brought the bottle and the Japanese crackers in a green-glazed bowl. I ended up sitting on this silvery chair, at a spindly round metal table, looking out over the red lights of Sutton.

'Kevin, I just want to say... there's nothing remotely conclusive on that tape. I have no doubt that what you can see moving there is only a man, or a man in a suit, just like the other film looks to me like a man in a bear-suit.'

'You keep telling me that I can't insist things are like they are just to fit with me. You do exactly the same.'

'Kevin, I have thousands of years of scientific method on my side. You have shouting and the cracker-barrel philosophising of a Satanist.'

'He prefers "demonologist".'

'Does he?'

'No, I made it up, like I make everything up.'

'You need to prepare yourself for the eventuality that tomorrow this all turns out to be an elaborate hoax.'

'It won't. It can't.'

'Kevin, none of this is making you happy. I don't know what it is, but you've staked too much of yourself on this whole Giganto thing. It's probably to do with something unpleasant and painful that happened to you once, something I can help you with if you want me to help you. I mean, I don't know anything about you beyond your obsessions and what they have cost you. You've never mentioned your mother, your father, any brothers or sisters, any friends other than Derek or Edward – any girlfriends other than your wife, who I only know you met by Internet dating as she told me so. Are you seeing anyone at the moment? Do you have a significant other?'

'I'm still technically married.'

'So you're a stickler for the rules. Why's that? What was your childhood actually like, Kevin?'

'I was raised by a kindly she-ape called Kala, in Beddington Park, in the little grotto bit near Henry's Table. We used to watch the wedding parties and the pissheads fighting from under the bushes. Sometimes we'd go and piddle in their lager-and-limes—'

'Tell me, when did you first start seeing things?'

'I don't see things, Max. I *know* things.'

'Have you ever had any sort of head injury? Have you ever experienced anything you would say was a crisis?'

I was trying to read between the lines here. I was trying to follow the base code, the subtext, and as The Funnel so rightly says, sometimes the subtext overwhelms the text, bursts forth and swamps it.

FACT: I didn't try to take her hand. I was swatting a mosquito that looked like it was about to bite her.

FACT: I only tried to peck her on the cheek because it

looked like she wanted to repay me for saving her from the mosquito.

FACT: I didn't deserve a slap but I'm big enough to let it go.

FACT: I didn't run out. I was going anyway.

❯ • ❮

On the way home, I realised who her stare had reminded me of. It was someone from a book. A woman in a book I'd read many years ago, when I was a kid. A character in a book that had scared me so much that I wouldn't be able to read the book again, even now. It wasn't *The Rats* by that James Herbert, or *Jaws*. Her stare was the same as the Lady of the Green Kirtle in *The Silver Chair* by C.S. Lewis. The Lady of the Green Kirtle can turn into a green serpent that can hypnotise gnomes and children into doing stuff they don't really want to do. The Lady of the Green Kirtle imprisons the prince underground. The Lady of the Green Kirtle almost succeeds in convincing the children that Narnia isn't real. This was what I was up against; had been all my life. Tomorrow, one of us was going to be proved right – and it wasn't going to be her.

GIGANTOPITHECUS INTELLIGENCE TEAM

REPORT #214 (CATEGORY A)

SECTION 7

Report on Field Trip II/ (i)

<u>GIT Investigators</u>

Lead Investigator: Maxine Cash
Secondary Investigator: Kevin Stubbs
Cryptozoologist: Derek Funnel

Accompanied by: Primary Witness X

Hoping to make the most of the light, Secondary Investigator Stubbs and I collected the witness at 18.00. However, there was some delay in leaving the property due to a dispute about money and the witness's reservations about GIT Cryptozoologist Funnel. Secondary Investigator Stubbs and I, accompanied by the witness, finally arrived at Banstead Common at 19.15.

Post-slap, I can't say I was exactly looking forward to seeing Sci-Borg on the night of the site investigation. As planned, after work I flew by her service-portal and collected her. She was fully costumed-up: one-piece pistachio-green cycling costume; protective goggles; the crap tablet she uses for field investigations under her arm. Abe Sapien, the fishman from *Hellboy*. He was part fish, part C3PO. It came back to me then that he was who she reminded me of when she wore her ops outfit. I didn't tell her that, though. We didn't speak. It was like being with Boho, except Boho, to her credit, never made me turn off the 'Theme from *King Kong*' when we were driving. I gunned the Abominable and headed back to the St Helier estate to pick up The DJ.

When we pulled up outside the house, she told me that all day she'd been trying to phone The DJ but he hadn't answered. He didn't know we were coming.

'If he doesn't let us in,' she said, 'we'll draw a line under this.'

'Don't you worry, Scully,' I said. 'I've got an enforcer in the back of the van.'

'Kevin, why on earth do you even own an enforcer?'

'I'm from Sutton.'

I got out of the van and slammed the door, hard.

On the doorstop, she knocked, and The DJ opened.

'Oh look, it's the Gay Team.'

'I'll get the enforcer,' I said.

'Kevin, are you blind? He's already opened the door.'

We follow him inside and Sci-Borg says, 'Mr Brunt, we have now had opportunity to assess the film you shared with us yesterday. It is very interesting, but we'd like you to take us back to where you saw what you say you saw, so we can run further tests and analytics. Would you be amenable to that?'

'Bollocks. That's worth six grand. You lot shoved it on the Internet for nada.'

'I assure you that we didn't, Mr Brunt.'

'It weren't me,' said The DJ. 'Must have been you lot.'

'Mr Brunt, no way would we have broken our promise to you.'

'Only me and you had it.'

'We will only take an hour of your time, Mr Brunt?'

The DJ seemed confused by this line of argument, especially as he knew in his low-storage battery that he didn't flush his six grand down the khazi.

'Where's that freak?' said The DJ. 'That freak done our bird table.'

'I very much doubt that,' said Sci-Borg.

'Only a gigantopithecus has the strength,' I chipped in.

'Does the giant prickus know how to use a bleeding hacksaw?'

'Mr Brunt—'

'And Freakboy nicked this clown pendant I bought for Summer. It's worth a grand, that is. If I'm going with you, I want six K for the film and a K for the clown.'

'Mr Brunt, don't you think it would be much better if you just came with us.'

'Piss off.'

'Then we can find out whether what you saw was real or not.'

'Don't care.'

'Wouldn't it be better if you had this off your mind?'

'Do one.'

'Wouldn't it be better for your children, who you say were scared by the event, if we were able to prove once and for all that this is all a misunderstanding?'

'Leave my kids out of it.'

'Mr Brunt, if the footage does turn out to be genuine, if we find evidence, any monies accruing from it are yours, I assure you.'

This was a step too far. She was acting like Gaddafi when he gave up his nuclear arsenal just so he could have a bunk-up in the desert with Tony Blair. And look what happened to the so-called Brotherly Leader after that?

'Listen, mate,' I said, 'get in the van before I call up The Freak and get him to smear Sunpat Crunchy all over your bird, see if we can bring Mohammed to the mountain. They love a bit of crunchy, especially the really gigantic ones.'

'Kevin!'

'All right,' said The DJ, 'but I want her pendant back.'

'Deal.' I shook his hand.

'Boys,' said Sci-Borg, 'let us proceed with some decorum, please. And you, Mr Stubbs, calm down.'

I looked at The DJ and he looked at me. We raised our eyebrows, like we'd shared something together, that we were talking the same language. The DJ had come down from seven grand to a clown pendant worth twenty-five pence. We were not going to tell Summer that, Scout's honour.

〉•〈

I got the witness-to-history into the back of the van. As soon as I pulled off, he started to have some sort of panic attack.

'It's horrible, horrible. I keep seeing it. At night, when I close my eyes, I feel it looming over me.'

'That's Summer, you tool,' I said.

'It's got a triangle for a head.'

'Don't worry,' said Sci-Borg. 'I can assure you that you won't see it again.'

'You promise?'

Before she could answer, I whacked on the CD player and 'Theme from *King Kong*' at full blast. Thought a bit of loud Geoff Love might calm him down as we headed for Banstead Common and the Great Confirmation.

GIGANTOPITHECUS INTELLIGENCE TEAM

REPORT #214 (CATEGORY A)

SECTION 7

<u>Report on Field Trip II/ (ii)</u>

The witness took us to the exact spot of the sighting. He reiterated his account, explaining that around 21.00 on 6 July, co-witness Dawkers had first seen the subject and then attributed a motive to the subject. When other co-witnesses had started to scream, the subject had moved across the treeline, smashing a log against the tree trunks, vocalising and possibly singing a song, although this time the witness remembered that the subject had thrown a large flint at the party before pausing in the gap in the trees to make a V-sign before disappearing in the direction of the Brighton Road and Banstead Downs Golf Course.

REPORT #214:
THE FACTS BY KEVIN STUBBS:
SECTION SEVEN (II)

When we arrived, saying bollocks to any bylaws and the Highway Code I went off-road and sped the Abominable right across the Common towards the site. It was dead easy to locate. In front of some trees was a great crop-circle-sized pattern of lager cans. I'd seen those trees before. Those trees were in the 'Banstead Bigfoot' film, a Category A sighting. These trees were already legend.

I killed the engine. I was lit-up now, lit-up inside like a guy on Bonfire Night. I got out of the van and sprung The DJ, leaving Sci-Borg to keep an eye on him while I climbed back in and loaded myself up with the kit.

Sample jars for hair and scat: CHECK.

Plaster of Paris kit for casting tracks: CHECK.

Camcorder: CHECK.

Cameras: CHECK.

Sci-Bionic Parabolic Microphone and Short Range Listening Device, aka The Sonic Scream, for recording howls or wood knocks: CHECK.

Two grand's worth of thermal imaging camera, aka The Heat Ray: CHECK.

Wraparound aviator shades: CHECK.

Enforcer: LEAVE IN VAN.

Bung it all on.

Gigantopithecus, ROAR.

I sprang from the back of the Abominable, and with

the camcorder took a one- hundred-and-eighty-degree scan of the site. We were westside, close to the Brighton Road. I could still hear traffic. To the east, a great expanse of grass stretched out towards Sutton Lane. Not a lot of cover, but this beast was smart, smarter than us, smarter than me. I tilted the lens and filmed the grass for a bit, a technique I'd learned watching Sasquatch sighting videos on YouTube. The Yanks always do this. There must be something in it. I scanned the trees. Those trees. It must be in the trees.

Through the viewfinder, I saw that Sci-Borg and The DJ had gone on ahead. They were walking towards the crop circle of lager cans, nattering like old mates. As if by magic, The Funnel appeared at my shoulder.

'Jesus' tits,' I said. 'You scared the crap out of me.'

'Shhh, Mr Stubbs, the readings are high. There's a disturbance in the field.'

'Where have you been? I've been trying to call you, like, all day.'

'Let us go gently into this eldritch night.'

'Here, did you nick The DJ's missus's clown-thing?'

He didn't answer and strode away, heading towards the crop circle of cans. The other two had paused there. The Funnel's Swedish army jacket flapped on the slight breeze. The fading sunlight caught his wild hair. For a second, apart from the fact that it had The Funnel in it, the scene looked like one of those Dutch sunflower paintings in that calendar Boho hung on our kitchen wall when she was pregnant with Kyrylo.

I filled up. I wanted him here, Kyrylo. I wanted him to see this: to see me here, witness to history.

I'm glad I was wearing wraparound aviator shades. I didn't want Sci-Borg or The DJ to see I'd been grizzling.

As I yomped over towards the cans where the others were standing, I filmed the grass and some random shots of treetops and sky, trying to make the camerawork as shaky as possible. Any Category A footage would look even more authentic now.

The DJ shoved The Funnel in the chest. Sci-Borg, rather than actually doing anything, turned sideways and slapped her own forehead.

I am a Knower, right. I get my hands dirty. I was up to my elbows in it as soon as I arrived, doing my Kofi Annan King Solomon bit, putting myself between the two of them.

'Leave it out,' he said. 'Where's the clown?'

'Give him the clown, Del.'

'What clown?'

'The clown you nicked yesterday.'

'How dare you? I've never stolen anything in my life.'

'We both saw you with it last night,' said Sci-Borg.

'I have many things. They have purposes.'

'I know bigger blokes than him.' The DJ nodded at me but he was talking to The Funnel.

I nodded to The DJ, but I was talking to Sci-Borg. 'Look, this spanner's a scrote. Can't trust him.'

'Kevin, we can both see it in broad daylight.'

She reached over and lifted the pendant over The Funnel's head and bouff.

The Funnel fell to his knees, his face the colour of a turnip or the inside of a pear.

'No more foolish statement was ever made about me.'

'You're mental,' said The DJ.

'For once, I agree,' said Sci-Borg. 'Actually, not for once. Now, Mr Brunt, can you please go over again what happened here on Saturday night?'

One thing was certain: his posse certainly had a bit of a dingdong up here on the Saturday night. So much aluminium lay on the grass it felt like we were crash site investigators, not the GIT. It looked like something had fallen from the stars on the 6th of July. If I didn't know any different, I'd say that Giganto had arrived here inside a meteor, like at the beginning of *Superman*.

I let The DJ speak. He went over the whole thing again. As he repeated the FACTS about Saturday night, he started to shiver and shake. He was out of his comfort zone. No poxy clown or posse of blokes who drink in The Churn was going to save him out here. It was time for the GIT to come into its own.

He did now say something new.

'It lobbed this flint, right, and it made a gesture as it passed, with its paw, like it was threatening or judging us or something.'

Sci-Borg started tutting and frowning when The DJ added these two salient points.

The Funnel and I know, though, that remembering honestly is not an exact science, and a random level of detail comes back to you after a sighting. The 'shatting-up' effect of the first encounter dies down but then rears up again, especially if you revisit the site of the trauma, as The DJ was doing here.

It's not unknown for a gigantopithecus to make a hand gesture. They do have hands, with white palms. The legend, Gorgo Gartree, had seen one make a hand gesture while he himself was doing a funny handshake with a top copper on the golf course (this is an action that The Funnel thinks is a coded warning, telling Gorgo to stay away from freemasons who are lizardmen-in-disguise). That golf course is only over the road from here, so it was probably the same gigantopithecus that The DJ saw on 6 July.

That The DJ was embellishing his story and adding bits to it that we'd not heard before and couldn't see on the film meant that it was all becoming more real to him, and therefore to us in the process.

The light was beginning to fade. I could smell grass and foliage and pigeons cooed in the trees and the distant hush of traffic. The trees were ahead. There was a path there where great size-twenty feet with dermal ridges had recently trod, and would do so again. I was so laden down with kit. I had been waiting for this moment for all my life.

Face FACTS: I come from Sutton. I work in IT. I work for a company that rents skips. I live on the St Helier estate. I know Derek Funnel. My wife left me. I've been alone with a woman only three times since, and got slapped each time. And one of those times I wasn't even alone. I was in The Dog with that Janine from Merton after I'd paid for her to see Hominid Rex. I'm not allowed to see my boy. There's nothing on the telly anymore. All the good things are dying. All the little people out there are sheep. All the great men – like Jackie Hogg and Arthur C. Clarke – are dead. I live only for this. I live only to See, to Know. I live to be a part of the only legend left. I am weighed down by secret knowledge of how the world really works. I am weighed down by kit.

I am weighed down by the kit of life.

I said something dramatic, something that could have been used in the title sequence of the GIT TV series if Gorgo had ever got it off the ground.

I said, 'It's in the trees, it's coming.'

The others were not listening. They had moved off to look for the flint.

GIGANTOPITHECUS INTELLIGENCE TEAM

REPORT #214 (CATEGORY A)

SECTION 7

<u>Report on Field Trip II/ (iii)</u>

We could find no flint in the grass to test for prints or DNA, although there was plenty of evidence that there had indeed been a barbecue on 6 July.

It was bang out of order for Sci-Borg to wander off without telling me. When I caught up with her, the first thing she said was – and she said it all forlorn, like she was worried about me when I knew she was having an orgasm inside – she said, 'There's no flint, Kevin.' (Not, note, 'We can't find the flint *yet*, Kevin.')

'If some dippy spanner hadn't bunged the footage up on YouTube,' I said, 'there'd still be a flint.'

'Yeah,' said The DJ.

'I was talking to you, not her. One of your mates has been up here and had it as a souvenir.'

'Bollocks,' said The DJ. 'My mates don't nick stones.'

'It's far more likely,' said Sci-Borg, 'that no flint was thrown in the first place.'

'The other explanation,' said The Funnel, 'is that it came back.'

'Jesus H,' said The DJ. 'It can come back?'

'It came back to retrieve the flint, knowing that otherwise we would find the flint and make its presence known. That's also why it damaged your bird table. It was warning you.'

'Shit. Shit.'

'I assure you, Mr Brunt,' said Sci-Borg, 'that even should the creature exist, which it does not, no primate behaves in this manner. Its consciousness could not be that evolved.'

'It always covers its tracks,' said The Funnel. 'That's why we never find anything.'

'That is the worst kind of woolly, magical thinking,' said Sci-Borg. 'There's no evidence so there must be a conspiracy.'

We were so locked into the sort of deep, measured back-and-forth discussion that takes over when you're on a Field Trip that none of us realised, until now, that The DJ had turned an ashen blue colour and his eyes had glazed.

'It's coming back,' he stammered. 'It's coming back. It's got a triangle for a head.'

I let Sci-Borg deal with it. She muttered something to me as she led The DJ a little way off. I'd already trained the camcorder on the trees. The trees up ahead. The slight upward slope to the trees. Something had been in those trees. Those trees rippled in the breeze. Those trees made a rushing sound like a waterfall. It was starting to get dark. Behind me, The DJ sobbed like a child.

I am supposed to be a cell of one, and while I've been shat-up many times, I am not supposed to cry. Never. I didn't cry when I first saw the gigantopithecus in the grounds of Morden Crematorium. Or when Boho took my boy away. But I had a cry earlier, back there on the field, and in Gorgo's conservatory when he passed me over. Something was up with me, something I didn't get. Maybe it was just getting to me, how big this thing was turning out to be, and how high the stakes.

GIGANTOPITHECUS INTELLIGENCE TEAM

REPORT #214 (CATEGORY A)

SECTION 7

<u>Report on Field Trip II/ (iv)</u>

I sent GIT Cryptozoologist Funnel up into the trees to re-enact the movements of the subject, and instructed Secondary Investigator Kevin Stubbs to camcorder the re-enactment. GIT Cryptozoologist Funnel paused at the subject's initial position so we could ascertain its size, then he walked across the treeline, impersonating the now-famous 'Giganto gait'.

We then reconvened to compare the re-enactment footage with the 6 July footage.

When paused at the subject's initial position, and when compared with the footage, we could ascertain that the subject was only two or three inches taller than Mr Funnel (who is 5' 6" in height). This contradicts the witness's statement that the subject was 'bigger than one of those basketball players you get in the States'. From a distance of some twenty feet and taking into account the poor light and general high spirits of the party on 6 July, I concluded that the subject of the footage was more likely a man than a cryptid.

We left the witness at the site of the barbecue, explaining to him that we needed him to stay there as a distance marker.

I was still filming the trees when as if by magic The Funnel appeared wearing night-vision goggles.

'Analysis,' I said.

'Mr Brunt is undergoing the Believer's Rite. Unlike you and I when we were first initiated, he's not a child. His mind cannot cope.'

'Not that. Giganto?'

'Oh he's been here. The question is—'

'—is he still here?'

I've never liked this civil partnership/finishing-each-other's-sentences malarkey that often characterises my relationship with The Funnel, but sometimes it saves time.

'I'm going up to the copse,' said The Funnel. 'We'll do the size comparison while Mr Brunt is still—'

'I'll go.'

I handed him the camcorder. I always do the size comparison. In fact, I positively love the size comparison. I love going up into the trees to mimic the walk or stance of the gigantopithecus so it can be measured to the scale of objects described in the witness report or visible in the photograph or the footage.

The Funnel wouldn't take the camcorder.

'I'll go,' he said.

'Not being funny or anything, mate, but you're a short-arse.'

'But Maxine says—'

'—you're a devil worshipper. That's well out of order, if you ask me.'

'Pardon me?'

'Maxine. Says you worship the devil. That you follow some Gary Crowley bloke who used to worship the devil.'

His jaw dropped. He went white, put his hand over his mouth and took a step backwards.

'Frakk me. It's true, isn't it?'

'Kevin, you and she are throwing old stones.'

'That still means it's true, don't it?'

'Setting aside that Gary Crowley is a DJ—'

'What? Like Brunt?'

'No. Not like Brunt. *Aleister* Crowley was an occultist, not a Satanist.'

'What's the difference?'

'It was Crowley who first alerted me to the significance of this event. He said that to quest for yetis, you have to violate every principle of science, decency and intelligence. You must be obsessed with an insane idea of the importance of the petty object of your wretched and selfish desires.'

'So Sci-Borg Max is talking out of her test tube as usual?'

'Maxine is casting the old slur her ilk have always cast.'

'And he was into this thing of ours, he was one of us?'

'Us is one of me. I will become when the alignments are right, on our return from the other side. On that score, Kevin, you must aid me in recovering the amulet.'

'Leave it out with that frakking clown.'

'Take a closer look at it. It has red eyes. A conical cranium. No neck. Dangling arms. I've seen one before, in Nepal. It opens the Gate.'

'Del, you get 'em in Argos. If you keep talking like that, Sci-Borg'll put the kibosh on this op. And you sure you want to go up for size comparison, mate? What if it's there?'

'Let me remind you that I have crossed swords with the Grey Emperor of Meldrogongkar.'

I watched him trudge up the slope towards the trees. Behind me, The DJ had stopped going mental and sparked up a fag. Sci-Borg was never going to be too impressed with this and sauntered over to me.

'You been doing your bit?' I said.

'He's confused.'

'He won't be soon.'

'I wish I had your positive vibes.'

'Del's not a devil worshipper. I just had a word with him.'

'Well, that's something.'

'Apparently, there's a difference between an occultist and a Satanist.'

'Kevin, I think maybe we should abort this investigation. The witness is getting distressed.'

'You can't. Look, Del's in the trees. Get DJ Gav. Confirm that's the right place.'

The DJ appeared. He didn't look distressed to me, merely hungover.

'It was further over,' he said. 'See that tree third from the end? He needs to go under that. There's that weird branch, like, I don't know, half a U-bend or something. It were under that.'

I waved at The Funnel and he moved to under the half-a-U-bend-shaped branch.

'Hold it, Del,' I called out. 'Hold it there, son.'

The Funnel stood on his tiptoes and steepled his fingers over his head.

I filmed about ten seconds of this before I instructed The Funnel to shift.

'Lope, Del. That's right, lope... like I showed you... over to that gap, between the two big 'uns. That's right, mate. Lope. Lope.'

I really should have been up there. I'd studied the Gartree-Hogg films ten thousand times. I'd perfected that walk. There was a time when I'd been practising so hard to imitate the Gartree-Hogg Sutton Cock Gigantopithecus that in the end I couldn't help doing it. It's dead hard. No human being apart from me walks in that way. I actually walk a bit like a gigantopithecus all the time now. I have to concentrate to be normal.

I think this is one of the reasons I got off to such a bad start with Boho. When I first met her in the Arrivals lounge at Heathrow, I was neck-stiff, knees limp, arms swinging, giant strides. After about four months her English was good enough to explain that she felt I should have told her I walk like a gigantopithecus in my emails.

The Funnel was doing his best, but his lope was, quite frankly, not what I'd ordered. He may have eaten a dead fish with a yeti, but he was mincing like a tit up there.

Anyway, I was trying to train the camera on the mince or wobble that was going on up there in the trees when The DJ started up.

'I've seen you before,' he said. 'In The Churn. You're the one they call the Monkey Man.'

Before I could say, 'Magic,' there's a thump. He collapses.

He was writhing on the grass, both hands clasped to his knee. Lying next to his trainer there was a dirty great flint, smooth and shaped like a tusk.

I looked at Sci-Borg and she looked at me and we both looked over to the trees. Just for a second I thought that this might actually be it, but it was only The Funnel there, in the gap, waving his hand.

'Sorry,' he called over. 'Just trying to be as accurate as possible.'

Sci-Borg started getting all headmistressy.

'Derek, come back here. Now. Come back here.'

The Funnel was mincing down the slope. The DJ got to his feet.

'One call,' he said. 'That's all it'll take. One call and Dawkers'll be here. We'll have him.'

'You threaten him again,' I told The DJ, 'and you're going to be the only one who knows where your body is buried.'

'How's that work then?'

'Time out,' said Sci-Borg. 'Will you all please behave?'

'Because of you two and your unprofessional behaviour,' I said, 'I only filmed him by the tree. We'll have to start again.'

'No, no, no,' said Sci-Borg. 'The tree will have to do.'

She got her powder-puff of a tablet out (I told her not to get that one, diabolical battery and screen-glare) and once The Funnel had joined us and things had been sufficiently choreographed so that Sci-Borg was acting as a Berlin Wall between The DJ and us, we started to have a look at a still of the 6 July gigantopithecus standing under the half-a-U-bend-shaped branch, side by side with The Funnel standing in the exact same spot with fingers steepled to impersonate a cone-shaped head.

I was in awe. I'd say that I'd never seen anything like this, but I had. Even so, I was still in awe. I was always in awe of it. Then Sci-Borg spoilt everything by placing the tips of her thumb and forefinger above The Funnel's image, then she moved them over to the Category A sighting. Here, she widened the gap between finger and thumb a tiny bit and said, 'The subject is only marginally taller than Derek.'

'No it's not,' I said. 'It's gigantic.'

She zoomed in on both images, so they became even more smeary, and again used her highly scientific pinch technique.

'If the 6 July subject was as large as Mr Brunt reports, its head would be peeping over the top of my finger.'

'What does he know?'

'Look, when Derek stands next to the tree, you can see the curved branch isn't that high up. It's probably about two metres, I'd guess.'

'This isn't about guessing, is it? You taught us that.'

'Mr Brunt, I think we can rest assured that what you saw is too short to be anything other than a man, whether he's wearing a suit or not.'

'Don't listen to her,' I said. 'This proves nothing. I should have gone up there. Del can't pull it off, he's hunched up.'

'It doesn't matter,' said Sci-Borg. 'We now know the height of the branch. The subject's head is a long way from the branch. Even at 208, 213 centimetres – say seven foot, quite small for a gigantopithecus, according to you two – it would reach the branch.'

'It's a baby one, then. They do have baby ones. There's one up in Nottingham Forest, and there's that film of Edward Heath—'

'Hearsay,' said Sci-Borg. 'Scandalous and preposterous hearsay. Mr Brunt, do you feel more assured now?'

'Does this mean it was that freak that did over my bird table?'

'For the last time,' said The Funnel, who had this purple face on, as if he was about to cast a spell, raise an army of the medieval undead of Sutton or something.

'We haven't even heard what Derek has to say about this,' I said.

I'll admit here that I was trying to draw some heavy artillery to my side. Sometimes you have to do this if you're up against inside-the-box thinking. They teach you that in IT. I learned it at college.

Sci-Borg huffed. 'Mr Funnel. Do you have anything to add regarding the height of the branch?'

'I see all ways. Futures, pasts. I am above you and in you. My ecstasy is in yours. My joy is to see your joy.'

'Weirdo,' said The DJ. 'Look at the 'kin state of you.'

'Shhh,' said Sci-Borg. 'Derek? Tell us what you think, and then we can pack up.'

The Funnel stroked his chin and stared into the trees as if mesmerised by something winking in and out of focus up there.

'I agree that the films may suggest that the beast is a little small for a gigantopithecus—'

Arsehole. Just when I needed someone to tell it as it is with the evidence of his own eyes.

'—but I'm generally suspicious of footage,' he said. 'The creature disrupts the electromagnetic field. How common is it, and I'm sure Mr Stubbs will corroborate this, that right at the moment you've got a gigantopithecus in your viewfinder, the battery fails, the camcorder shuts down, the focus settings change all of their own accord? These creatures interfere with electrical equipment at will. My conclusion is that on 6 July the creature was taller than it appears in the footage. What we see now has more in common with a shadow cast by time's arrow, or surface ripples on the glassy millpond of reality.'

'Derek, are you sure?' said Sci-Borg. 'Are you sure you've actually processed what just came out of your mouth.'

'It's the age-old human dilemma,' said The Funnel. 'You want to know it. It won't be known.'

'Fuck this,' said The DJ. 'I'm skinning up.'

'The other thing,' I said, 'is that we didn't compare the walk. With the best will in the world – no disrespect, Del – you walk more like, I don't know, a leprechaun or a Time Bandit or something. If we film the walk again, if I do it, we'll see that what he saw on 6 July could only be a gigantopithecus.'

'We have just proved,' said Sci-Borg, '*proved* using basic maths, basic mathematics, basic mathematics they teach you in school, basic mathematics that *I* teach in school, that the blotch on this film is man-sized. Now you want me to take into account something we haven't even seen?'

At this, for some reason, The DJ, now brandishing a jazz cigarette the size of a rolled-up copy of *The Sun*, let out this throaty cackle, his eyes now as red as Giganto's and as round as a very massive owl's.

'I think this is over,' said Sci-Borg. 'I think this is all over.'

'It's got a triangle for a head,' said The DJ.

'He did report that it vocalised,' said The Funnel.

'I've heard enough,' said Sci-Borg. 'I've heard enough and I've seen enough. This case is closed.'

'Look,' I said, adopting my UN peacekeeper's role and nodding at The DJ. 'Why don't we ask him what he wants us to do? He got us out here after all.'

'Kevin, he's either going to agree because he's desperate for non-existent money, or he's going to scare the other half of himself to death.'

'It can happen,' said The Funnel. 'It can be a good thing. Why fear the tearing the of the veil?'

'I saw it,' said The DJ. 'It smelled like dog mess as well. You go on up there and have a butcher's. I need this thing out of my head.'

Sci-Borg was looking more uptight and boxed-in by FACTS than I've ever seen her. This wasn't over. This was just the beginning. Sometimes you have to be tenacious.

'Stay here,' Sci-Borg told The DJ. 'We can use you as a distance marker.' He flopped to his knees then onto his back, and looked up at the sky with the jazz fag held across his chest. Meanwhile, the GIT trudged up the slope towards the trees, Sci-Borg resigned and silent.

GIGANTOPITHECUS INTELLIGENCE TEAM

REPORT #214 (CATEGORY A)

SECTION 7

<u>Report on Field Trip II/ (v)</u>

The wooded area proved to be no more than a strip of trees, perhaps the remains of an ancient hedge that had divided estates or farmlands during the Middle Ages. A flattened track between the trees roughly corresponded with the transit of the subject. The track suggests that dog walkers, golfers and ramblers heading for the nearby Brighton Road or the golf course use the area as a shortcut. The ground turned out to be moist, not tough, with a thick leaf carpet beneath the trees. Shoe and boot prints were visible, but no large bipedal animal tracks. There was some evidence that the ground had been recently disturbed: slashes to the track made by some sort of stick or spade. An inspection of the trees found no unusual scratches or branch-snaps. We found no unusual hair samples caught on surrounding bushes or the trees' lower branches. We detected no odour in the woods incommensurate with an area used to walk dogs. We also did not find the pornographic title mentioned by the witness in his 8 July report. Secondary Investigator Stubbs traced the steps of the subject as recorded in the 6 July footage for reference.

GIT then rejoined the witness at the site of the barbecue.

REPORT #214:
THE FACTS BY KEVIN STUBBS:
SECTION SEVEN (V)

The way she describes 'the flattened track' in Report #214 makes it seem boring, that it was dull standing where only a few days before a gigantopithecus had roamed and roared. By the time we arrived up there I was already in the zone, trying to put my head into the mind of the gigantopithecus as it lumbered through on Saturday night. I imagined myself nine foot tall and having supersensitive senses and the stealth skills of a ninja or SAS commando. I turned my head really slowly, as if I was big and ominous, maybe even a machine that's part of nature, and looked back down the slope. I tried to imagine what Giganto saw on the Saturday night: a heaving mass of humanity making a dirty great racket. All I could see now was our 'distance marker', The DJ. He was spread-eagled on the grass. He could have been dead, if you didn't know he was whacked out of his bonce on jazz fags.

My super-surveillance senses tingled. Sci-Borg was close behind me, so I turned, and in doing so felt myself retract to human size.

'It clearly found its way here from a south-easterly tack,' I said. 'It used these trees as cover, blended in—'

'Pardon.'

'You know. Found his place in the woods.'

'I don't know what you're talking about.'

'I was thinking that they had kids up here, and if they had

peanut butter sandwiches, or bagels… but look at him down there. He probably thinks a bagel is a dog.'

As if by magic, The Funnel appeared.

'Mr Stubbs believes that the creature may want to take you as his wife. It is not unknown for the Visitors to mate with homo sapiens females.'

'Derek, this is intrusive and offensive. Now, let's get this over with. Animal behaviourist hats on, please. I'm sure Mr Brunt is desperate to get back to his children. What do we think of the terrain?'

'Perfectly in keeping with the sort of places we've traditionally seen the gigantopithecus,' I said, because it is. No doubt about it, FACT.

Sci-Borg made a revealing gesture. She stepped backwards, still looking at us, and swiped the air with her pinched forefinger and thumb. It was like she was about to write a list of instructions on a blackboard.

'I dispute that. There are hardly any trees here. This is a coppice, not a forest. Why would it come up here when there's nowhere for it to retreat? How would it even get up here without being seen? Look: all around us, flat, open parkland. If it's this highly adapted, stealthy king of the woods, why would it come here, where people walk their dogs and play golf, if it doesn't want to be found? Why, when it realised there's a lot of threatening noise, did it reveal itself rather than blend into the trees? This is not even taking into account that the size comparison exercise revealed it was tiny.'

'It's probably a baby one,' I said, 'and it was trying to reach its dad over at the golf course. We know its dad hangs out over there.'

'We do, do we?'

'Eddie saw it there.'

'Edward only *says* he saw it. Animals aren't eccentric. They have reliable needs and patterns of behaviour, unlike Edward Gartree.'

'I agree,' said the Funnel. 'Except it isn't an animal. It may well have materialised here, came out of phase. You might not realise this, but this is a ley line that connects the Green Borough to Stonehenge, and one thing we do know is that Stonehenge was built by what Bronze Age man referred to as giants, what we would call gigantopithei.'

'Let's not get at cross purposes here, Derek.'

'Its purpose is unknown. Our purpose is to discover the purpose of these beings.'

'Bollocks,' I said. 'Our purpose is to prove it's real.'

'That's right, Kevin,' said Sci-Borg. 'Our purpose is to prove that it's real, or that it isn't real so you can get on with your life.'

'This is my life.'

'Occam's Razor. The most likely, straightforward explanation is the explanation.'

'How romantic,' said The Funnel. 'The sceptic will applaud our labours.'

'We're on the brink of the Great Confirmation here,' I said. 'All of science is going to change. Everything is going to change for the better, believe me. Believe in something bigger and better for once in your life.'

'Kevin,' said Sci-Borg. 'If you would only stop seeing some grand opportunity in all of this you could be reconciled with your wife, and then you might be happier.'

'Happier? Happier? How could I be any happier?' I said. 'I'm a Knower. C'mon Del, let's find his tracks.'

This is the lot of the hardcore Knower. I might be lonely. I might sometimes long to be sitting on the sofa between my wife and kid, beer in hand, pizza on the coffee table, *Bigfoot and the Hendersons* on the plasma; but loneliness is part of the kit. It's what you have to go through to get to the other side. It's a virtue, and in the end, they will come back to you if you are virtuous. This is what I was pinning my hopes on, anyway.

I turned my back on her and took a few strides. Rather than fall in line with me, The Funnel wandered off towards the trees on the other side of the track. He deployed his Trifield, aka The Tractor Beam. I could hear its gentle buzz.

Finally, I got to do some crouching and hardcore looking at the ground. As soon as I was down there her shadow fell over me.

'Are you all right, Kevin?'

'Looking for his tracks.'

'Hmmm… in the report, Mr Brunt says the ground was hard, but it's moist, quite a thick leaf litter, don't you see?' She glanced upwards. 'There's a heavy canopy up there.'

'So what? He's a DJ, for God's sake. Can't believe a word he says. Until you've seen a gigantopithecus you don't know what it's like to go mental.'

She dropped down, so she was face-to-face with me.

'Listen, Kevin, I was talking to Bohuslava the other day—'

'Not now, Max.'

'And she says she left because of all this, you on your knees in the woods.'

I'm not stupid. I did know this. Of course, I knew. This just wasn't the time for her to go all couples counsellor on me. It was getting in the way of me looking for a dirty great gigantopithecus and saving myself as well as everybody else.

I noticed a shape in the leaf carpet, an imprint, too rounded to be the paw of a dog or a fox and bigger than any man's foot. Sci-Borg was a wasp in my ear when I was trying to work. I was staring at the print, making the massive amount of calculations and observations that only the true Knower is capable of.

'Kevin, I'm talking to you.'

'You noticed this?'

'What I'm trying to say here is that she does want you back. It's not just my intuition. All she wants is for all this to end, for you to get this out of your head, so you can come home and be a father to Kyrylo.'

'Look down. It's in front of you.'

'Kevin, it's not real, the ape-man. Can't you see that?'

'There's one massive flaw in all that. Look at this dirty, great print.'

I swiped my hand over the evidence like I was serving up the swankiest, most succulent meal from the kitchens of the best restaurant in Epsom or Cheam. This was a gigantopithecus footprint, no doubt about it, FACT.

'There's clear evidence of a marked flexibility in the midtarsal joint. Midfoot pressure ridges there display a greater range of flexion at the transverse tarsal joint than a normal bloke's tarsus would permit. A heel impression is missing. It's clear that the hindfoot was lifted at the time of contact by the midfoot. Due to the damp terrain, the foot slipped backward, as shown by the toe slide-ins. A ridge of mud was pushed up behind the midtarsal area. This is a Category A gigantopithecus footprint. No doubt about it. You seem to be forgetting that it's real. It's not a hoax, or a twat in a suit, or a Beckham spectre—'

'Brocken, Kevin. Brocken spectre. It's a trick of the light. When you're up in the mountains, the low sun behind you can project your shadow onto the clouds.'

'I don't care. The gigantopithecus is real. And when I've made everyone realise it's real, my boy will come back to me all of his own, don't you get that? Not only will all human life make sense, but I'll be able to see my boy.'

'I do understand that you've staked a lot of yourself on this—'

'Not this again.' I was standing up now. 'Look. Look at the print.'

She slid her boot alongside it, paused, had a think and then said, 'It's too small. I'm only a size four and it's not that much bigger.'

'Look at its toes. No one has toes like that. They're like a gorilla's toes.'

She didn't have any comeback, at least not yet, and stood there staring as if there was something wrong with me.

As if by magic, The Funnel piped up from the other side of the track. I thanked God and all his yetis for The Funnel. He would distract Maxine from her poking and prying. We would get back to being proper GIT.

'Lead Investigator,' he said. 'I've found something, strange scratch marks on this tree.'

I watched as Sci-Borg strode over to him, her elbows weirdly jerking at a faster rate than her legs.

She poked her beak at the tree for no more than a second – which isn't a very scientific period of study, I have to add – and then scuttled back to me in exactly the same jerky fashion.

'Be careful,' I said. 'Don't disturb the ground.'

'Heidi is a slag,' she said.

'What?'

'She's a slag.'

'I wouldn't know. I've never met her.'

'That's what it says on the tree, gouged with a penknife.'

The Funnel was among us once more.

'You're dismissing this too readily, Lead Investigator. The creature uses diversionary tactics. It left that message precisely so we'd think it hadn't been here. Oh, and that is a gigantopithecus footprint, by the way.'

'It looks more like it's been left by one of those barefoot running shoes.'

'The toe-slides are too uneven around the edges,' I chipped in.

'Guys, there's only one print. Are you saying it hopped here on one flipping leg?'

'Unlikely,' said The Funnel. 'It's more likely that it dropped its shadow cloak here. The heel print was left behind in another dimension.'

'First you're saying it can write, now you're saying it bends the laws of physics?'

'I'd hazard that it can read, too. Where, for example, is the exotic publication Mr Brunt mentioned?'

'All that proves is that *men* have been up here.'

'Yes, and this site has clearly been tampered with,' said The Funnel. 'You can see that the track looks like it's been raked or slashed with a stick or a spade.'

'The DJ's mates came back, looking for trophies,' I said.

'Oh no, I suspect that the creature returned once it realised it had been seen by multiple witnesses. It covered its tracks and made the crude marks on the tree. I suspect it removed the exotic publication as well.'

'That's insane,' said Sci-Borg. She turned her back on us and walked away towards the 'Heidi is a slag' tree. She rested her forearms on its trunk and stayed there.

'Oh blow,' said The Funnel. 'Do you think we've upset her? Should I, you know, maybe go over and comfort her?'

'No, mate, you better not. Not you. I know how to cheer her up. Oi, Maxine... Maxine... Max... Maximillian... watch this.'

I waited until she'd clocked us. Then I heaved myself up to my full massive height, stiffened the old neck, let my arms dangle as much as they could dangle, then scuffed the ground with my huge feet and I panted and I growled and I launched myself in a well proper lope across the treeline, throwing my long arms back and forth. I was loping, proper loping, all that expertise I'd gathered from watching the Gartree-Hogg/ Sutton Cock footage for ten thousand hours burning through me.

When I reached the end of the track I slowed to a shamble. As I was catching my breath, I noticed a thick stick lying in the grass.

I picked it up, weighed it in my hand, and then, like I've done ten thousand times, I bunged it all on and whacked it squarely against a tree.

Ker-RACK!!!

The sound echoed around the woods. Birds flapped and spiralled upwards. The best wood knock ever reverberated across the London Borough of Sutton, and through time, back to Andreasweald, the dreaming forest of England, to stir the kindred spirit of the noble and elusive gigantopithecus. It knew that it was not alone. I was living in the air tonight, but I was feeling a bit guilty about Sci-Borg – I mean Maxine, aka Sci-Borg.

I know what it's like to be outflanked, to be confronted by sure-fire evidence you can't explain. I know what it's like to be passed over and shouted at and even belted by the opposite sex. I have, I must admit, acquired a great deal of respect and affection for her over the last few months. All relationships are based on slanging matches and verbals, at least in my experience.

I sauntered over. She was standing with The Funnel. He was pointing his Trifield at her in a way that was, I should imagine, not at all comforting. She took a rapid step towards me once I was close and gave me this smirky look.

'That was very impressive, Kevin,' she said.

'A solid knock,' said The Funnel. 'That should lure the beastie from its burrow.'

'I'll do the call if you like.'

'Guys, guys, guys, guys, guys,' said Sci-Borg. 'There's nothing here, is there? Can we just draw a line under this one and go and tell Mr Brunt we've not found anything?'

It was likely that she wanted to say a lot more here, a lot, lot more. It would go on for ages and ages and we'd have to listen to it. It would be as bad and as boring as having to read a nature book at school, like being kept behind after the bell, and the quiet of the classroom when there's nothing to do except read about the life cycle of the caddis fly larva. You open your mouth; they keep you back. You're bigger than the other kids, and the teachers think you're thick and weird anyway; they keep you indoors. You ask the wrong question at home; your mum keeps you indoors. Sometimes it's necessary to say the opposite of what you mean just to get a chance to play in the sun.

I looked at The Funnel. The Funnel looked at me.
'Yes,' we said, in unison, a cell of two.

GIGANTOPITHECUS INTELLIGENCE TEAM

REPORT #214 (CATEGORY A)

SECTION 7

<u>Report on Field Trip II/ (vi)</u>

GIT then discussed our findings with the witness. I was somewhat surprised when Secondary Investigator Stubbs and Cryptozoologist Funnel both told the witness that, there being no rational explanation for what he had seen, the subject of the footage could only be the gigantopithecus, also known as 'Giganto', or the 'Banstead Bigfoot'.

So, we left the woods and the oddly unremarked-upon gorilla-like footprint and headed down the slope towards The DJ and the crop circle of lager cans. The light was definitely weaker. The sun was going down.

'I'm so pleased,' said Sci-Borg, 'that for once we were able to use rational argument to reach a sensible conclusion.'

This was a smokescreen, obviously. She couldn't admit she was spooked up there. I know it must have been a bit awkward for her, a bit unsettling to be more or less alone in the woods with a gigantopithecus *and* The Funnel in close proximity.

I wondered about the ley-line business as well, and whether The Funnel picked up any readings with his Trifield, aka the Tractor Beam. I was wondering if there was anything in this, and that maybe the gigantopithecus did use electromagnetic energy to travel undetected and shat-up the kit.

I'd recently seen a video on YouTube of Russian Special Forces soldiers on a Siberian military base. They were surrounding this heat haze that looked a bit like Giganto. The bloke on the voice-over sounded like Boss Hogg from *The Dukes of Hazzard*. He said that if you wait until just before your mind can begin to play tricks on you, you can clearly see it's a Russian Bigfoot using cloaking technology from somewhere else in the universe.

I must admit that at the time I thought his analysis was the rantings of a piss artist. Now I was starting to think that this good old boy hadn't been talking a crock of bollocks after all.

'If we get this over with in a polite and professional fashion,' said Sci-Borg, 'I might let both of you buy me a drink.'

Any second I reckoned she was going to grab both our hands, swing them up into the air, and make us skip down the hill towards The DJ.

Anyway, we reached the old DJ, who was now on his feet, kicking at cans as if taking penalties at an invisible goal. We gave him a second. He didn't even look at us.

'Welcome to the club,' I said. 'There's no doubt that what you saw was a gigantopithecus.'

This gets his attention. When he looks up, his face is as grey as the face of the Grey Man of Ben MacDhui, Scotland's yeti. The Funnel once showed me a photograph of it that he bought from a Dutch nudist.

'You're shitting me,' said The DJ. 'Don't shit with me.'

'There's no other explanation. What you saw can only have been a gigantopithecus.'

'Kevin,' said Sci-Borg. 'For the life of me, I thought we'd agreed.'

'We did,' I said.

'Mr Brunt. I assure you, we found—'

'Burns on the grass,' said The Funnel, 'in keeping with the deployment of a teleportation disc or cloaking device on a high setting. It walks among us.'

'You see it? You see its head, the triangle?'

'I've seen its head many times,' I said. 'I interviewed this lady from Roundshaw once who regularly saw it peering through her window at night. There was a jar of Sunpat Crunchy in her fridge, you see. They don't like the smooth—'

'Oh no, no,' he said. 'I can't. I can't take it... can't get my head around this.'

'Kevin,' said Maxine, 'shut it, shut your... trap.'

'Mr Brunt,' said The Funnel. 'Be aware that it has now seen you. It knows that you know. It will have marked you out. It will keep its eyes on you. Do not be afraid, though. It is fashioned merely from the substances of shadow.'

The DJ started to claw at his chest like his sweatshirt was alive with lice. At which point, Sci-Borg erupted.

GIGANTOPITHECUS INTELLIGENCE TEAM

REPORT #214 (CATEGORY A)

SECTION 7

Report on Field Trip II/ (vii)

I then explained to the witness and Secondary Investigator Stubbs and Cryptozoologist Funnel that I believed there to be such a profound dearth of evidence that the sighting could only be dismissed as either a misidentification or an outright hoax. I cited the inconsistencies in the witness's account; that at the time of the sighting he may well have been under the influence of alcohol and recreational drugs; that his motive for contacting the GIT seemed to be financial rather than scientific. I reiterated my long-held reservations about the credibility of any of the earlier sightings of a relict hominid in this district, Edward Gartree being very much in the entertainment business and his partner Jack Hogg a costumier; that the area is both developed and the woodland extremely constrained, and thus a large, shy animal would have no reason to be here and have nowhere to go if cornered or threatened. I cited that the locomotion of the subject in the footage was inconsistent with that of a large primate; I explained that fossils show that the gigantopithecus was usually nine feet tall when the subject of the footage is approximately six feet tall; I cited that the red eyes seemed to be electrically generated, maybe part of a sportsman's cap or visor with

night-lights; I cited the lack of physical evidence at the site
and the signs that the site had been disturbed or swept in
some way; I explained that as the witness's party made a
great deal of noise, that they were in fact having an 'old skool
rave', they would have scared off any wild animals (deer,
etc.) for miles around, so it seems less than feasible that a
supposedly reclusive animal like a gigantopithecus would
approach the source of the noise. I explained that should
pockets of the gigantopithecus population have survived
extinction a hundred thousand years ago, a community of
at least ten thousand would be needed as breeding stock
to maintain itself, even in an area as small as the very-
densely-populated-by-very-aggressive-homo sapiens-for-
hundreds-of-years south-east of England; I also explained
that we live on a tiny island, so in no way could a species
of large primate remain elusive and free from captivity and
study by transmigrating across vast tracts of wilderness,
as is theoretically possible in the United States of America,
Siberia or China. I also explained that the gigantopithecus
never lived in Europe and is only known to have inhabited
China, India and Indochina. Furthermore, I mentioned that
England more or less invented taxonomy, with members of
the Victorian gentry scouring the countryside cataloguing
everything. It's hard to believe that they would have missed
a large primate. I also explained that most of the witness's
associates are parochial, of low intelligence, credulous and
probably criminals. The scientific community will not take
their testimony seriously.

It's not like I'd not heard her arguments before. It's not like I'd not heard them from a whole army of experts and deniers well before I'd met Sci-Borg. I'd heard them from Boho and the spanners in The Churn and the YouTube commentators like Fortean Tony and Man_in_a_Suit. Their voices were all fizz and static to me. You can't take any of their arguments seriously, not after you've seen a gigantopithecus with the evidence of your own eyes. All science does is make it 'unlikely' that there's a 'rectal hominid' (or whatever Sci-Borg calls it). It doesn't mean there isn't one.

Lots of things were unlikely, but they happened.

It was unlikely that the coelacanth (aka an old fish) had survived the prehistoric era but it did: FACT.

When Japanese sailors pulled a strange, massive and rotting sea creature from the Pacific, it was unlikely that it was a plesiosaur, but The Funnel says it was: FACT.

It was unlikely that my mum ever stayed in the same room with my dad, whoever he was (I still hope he was Arthur C. Clarke), long enough for her to work out how to get pregnant with me, but she must have done: FACT.

Everything is unlikely. Every day an unlikely thing happens.

And this day, today, here on the Common with Sci-Borg yapping, I could feel in the air tonight that something absolutely unlikely but absolutely FACTUAL was about to reveal itself. I didn't butt in. Instead, I was thinking what if everything she'd said was true, and tried to imagine what I'd be like if I didn't have the GIT and the gigantopithecus to hunt, what an empty sack of a life I'd be living.

I can remember very clearly the day that I first saw the Gartree-Hogg/Sutton Cock footage. It was just after I'd been discharged from hospital, after the Chelsea fans mugged me outside The Churn – the day Mum passed. I was studying for my BTEC in Computing, so I'd been at college earlier on the day she died. Marlon, the department administrator guy who looked a bit like Twiki from *Buck Rogers in the Twenty-Fifth Century* (I'd been catching up on this classic series at the time, having missed out on it first time round because it wasn't appropriate, obviously), had come looking for me just after lunch. He found me hiding in one of the toilet cubicles. There had been a phone call for me.

The thing is, in the months before the criminal assault I'd been getting a soppy feeling for this girl called Francesca. Nice smile. Long legs. Long hair. Always wore miniskirts and a faun suede jacket. Cheam, not Sutton; aka sophisticated. Everyone called her Frankie, but to be different and stand out I called her Franco. We were in the same classes, except she couldn't make any of them, so I used to share my notes and projects with her. We'd met for a cup of coffee once. I was sure at the time that I'd felt all her code downloading into mine and vice versa, with the emphasis on the vice.

Anyway, that morning I swaggered into the refectory, pretty sure I now had the conkers to ask her out. I, Kevin Stubbs, was going to ask a girl out – probably to The Dog in Carshalton, not The Churn, for obvious reasons. Straightaway I hear my name mentioned. I hear some girl say, 'that Kevin Stubbs'. No one else had noticed me, though. It was like I was wearing an alien cloaking device.

In the middle of the refectory was a square formation of orange sofas unofficially reserved for the so-called Clickers Clique, aka the cool set from Epsom and Cheam too smug to admit they weren't clever enough to go to university, who pretended that North East Surrey College of Technology was in *Beverly Hills 90210* and drove around in convertible Golf GTIs and wore white trousers and got off with each other.

I could see her long tawny hair as it dangled over the back of the sofa.

It's her.

Franco.

Franchescalicious.

This close, her blossomy smell tingled my face. I realised that Franco had said my name. She'd said, 'that Kevin Stubbs'.

Expecting that she would now coo an appreciation of how good I was at teaching her how to code and work with computerised systems, I was trying not to burst into tears of appreciation when she hunched up her shoulders.

'I was tempted... tempted or toyed?... I'm not sure. I toyed. Yes, that's it. I toyed with calling in the RSPCA. Even they call him the Skunky Gibbon, you know.'

One of her *Surrey Hills 90210* mates, this bloke with an earring and white trousers, called T'Pau or Reagan or something, was grimacing at her and jabbing a finger in my direction. I knew that he didn't care about my feelings; he was trying to save her from embarrassment, and improve his chances of having a rummage in her linen basket, probably.

'Someone needs to teach him how to wash,' she continued, 'and someone needs to explain to him that the flecky £5 Burton sale trousers are not a good look, especially not for someone who is more mound than man.'

When she looked up, she didn't flinch. An expression of gleeful spite radiated from her face.

Paralysed by the stare of the Lady of the Green Kirtles, I must have hid in the toilet cubicle for hours before Marlon the departmental admin found me and gave me the message from the hospice. I had a bad case of the Kirtles. I had Kirtles in my brain, in my guts. In league with the Red Darkness of Sutton, they followed me all the way to the hospice, then all the way to The Churn. After I was discharged from hospital, the Red Darkness and the Kirtles were in my head when I let myself into The Church of the Poisoned Mind, aka my mum's house. At home, I was alone with my Kirtles, alone with the Red Darkness rearing up behind me.

My cheek was still stinging when I switched on the TV. There it was, though, on the news, prowling across the screen: massive, hairy, with long swinging arms, red glowing eyes, a cone-shaped cranium and a look of 'serene and inhuman indifference'.

I knew straightaway.

There would be no more Red Darkness.

There would be no more Kirtles.

I would not be kept underground any longer.

No one would talk about me like that ever again.

No one would treat me as their punchbag for kicks.

There would be no more mooning over the Francos, not when such awesome magnificence still existed in Sutton and the world. I now knew my destiny. Arthur C. Dad had

first whispered it to me, but now he was shouting through a
megaphone: GO FORTH AND KNOW!

> • <

So, let's pause here. Let's rewind to the moment I'm alone in
the flat, alone with the Kirtles and the Red Darkness.

What if the TV was on the fritz?

What if I'd read a book instead?

Or taken a nap?

What if I'd never seen the Gartree-Hogg Footage?

Missed it.

Let it pass me by.

Could easily have missed it.

It was covered up afterwards.

There was a massive conspiracy to hide it from public
record.

What would it have been like for me if I'd not seen the
footage?

The quiet flat.

The Kirtles.

The sting.

Days would drag on until college ends.

Work starts.

The quiet flat.

I would work in IT and address problems and listen
to grey people talk of food and sleep and love and other
things and come home and sit in the quiet flat with the Red
Darkness and my Kirtles.

If it hadn't been for Giganto, I wouldn't even have met
Bohuslava.

She should know that.

If it hadn't been for Giganto, Kyrylo wouldn't have been born, born to ride with me through the forests of the Earth, all the forests where ape-like bipeds rip deer to shreds and shit-up campers.

Maybe I should have told Boho that I only found her because one night I was on YouTube, watching a one-hundred-per-cent Category A film of a Bigfoot falling over in a cornfield in Ohio, when I accidently clicked this popup advert for 'Meet Ukrainian Brides Now'.

I had other reasons for not telling her this.

I didn't want her to think I'd ordered her like a pizza.

Heartbreak pizza.

Fresh from Kharkov.

The quiet flat.

Alone with the Kirtles.

Or: out in the woods with two grand's worth of thermal imaging camera, aka the Heat Ray, a great bit of kit, howling the howl and whacking a tree with a stick. Up on the Downs. Over to Chipstead or Stoneleigh. Night-vision goggles and the Sci-Bionic Parabolic Microphone and Short Range Listening Device, aka the Sonic Scream (a great bit of kit).

You can't say that I haven't made something of myself.

You can't say I didn't get straight back up again and walk the walk, roar the roar.

And I don't blame anyone for anything, ever.

I don't.

This is what Sci-Borg cannot grasp.

This is not an emotional problem.

This has always been about finding the missing link.

The secret of life.

> • <

Anyway, all this was going through my head as Sci-Borg gave us the science yap.

GIGANTOPITHECUS INTELLIGENCE TEAM

REPORT #214 (CATEGORY A)

SECTION 7

<u>Report on Field Trip II/ (viii)</u>

None of these explanations convinced the witness. However, when I repeated the old Sherpa saying, 'There is a yeti in the back of everyone's mind and only the blessed are not haunted by it' (a line I have quoted to both Secondary Investigator Stubbs and Cryptozoologist Funnel on many occasions) and then tried to explain to the witness that he may have experienced pareidolia, he became so extremely irate that I feared he would now assault Cryptozoologist Funnel.

Like the rest of us, The DJ had shut down while Sci-Borg was giving us all a lecture; or he was still whacked out of his bonce on jazz fags. Throughout, he was glazed over. I was glazed over. The Funnel was glazed over. The sky over Banstead Common had glazed over.

It was only when Sci-Borg brought The DJ's mates into it that he perked up.

'My mates ain't criminals,' he said. 'Bobby Meakle runs the Chicago Rock.'

'That's beside the point,' said Sci-Borg. 'Look, there's an old Sherpa saying, "There is a yeti in the back of everyone's mind and the only the blessed are not haunted by it."'

'I fear a little wisdom can be dangerous in the wrong hands,' said The Funnel.

'Mr Brunt,' said Sci-Borg. 'Are you au fait with the term "pareidolia"?'

'There was one up at Rosehill. Dawkers paid him a visit.'

'No, not one of those. Parei-*dolia*. Like when you see a face in a tree trunk?'

'No.'

'Or like when someone reports they've seen Jesus in a, I don't know, a muffin?'

'No.'

At this point, The DJ shivered. He twitched his nose. He rolled his shoulders, one after the other, and looked down at himself.

I can't deny – I saw it with the evidence of my own eyes – that The Funnel did have his hand lodged in the pocket of The DJ's tracksuit bottoms.

So, The DJ shoved The Funnel in the chest.

The Funnel toppled backwards and released something from his hand. The clown amulet arced over his head and The Funnel ended up flat on his back on the grass.

I managed to get a weak grip on The DJ's elbow. I was carrying a camcorder, parabolic microphone and two grand's worth of thermal imaging camera, and had to strike out with my left hand. Sci-Borg stepped in and pulled back on his other arm, so his first kick was too high to connect with The Funnel's unmentionables. We wrestled The DJ. We tried to overpower him. We pulled him away. He went limp. He stopped. He looked up at the treeline. He went white.

White.

Proper.

Shat-up.

White.

GIGANTOPITHECUS INTELLIGENCE TEAM

REPORT #214 (CATEGORY A)

SECTION 7

<u>Report on Field Trip II/ (ix)</u>

I then realised that the witness was in some distress. The witness now took a step back from the team. He was pointing at the trees. He explained to us that 'it' was back. 'It' was up there in the trees.

At this point, GIT Cryptozoologist Derek Funnel was kneeling on the ground with his palms pressed to the grass, nodding his head rhythmically and reciting some sort of chant or prayer.

I must admit that what I saw standing in the trees astounded me. Unlike Secondary Investigator Stubbs and Cryptozoologist Funnel, I had never before experienced a close encounter with a gigantopithecus. Thus I could not empathise with the feeling of awe they had both described as consuming them during first-hand observations of the gigantopithecus. Until now, I could not relate to the oft-recounted feeling of awe an investigator will experience when, despite his or her prior reservations, scepticism and scientific training, he or she sees something out of time, that should not be. This feeling of awe, in previous reports, especially from the Gartree Era (see GIT Reports #1, #3, #8 and #14 in particular) is most epiphanic and disturbing the first time the investigator sees a gigantopithecus.

What I saw then was a gigantopithecus standing in the same gap in the trees where it pauses in the 6 July footage. As in the witness's report of 8 July, the gigantopithecus was tall, bulky, no-necked with a conical head, covered in black-brown hair, long-armed and with red, burning eyes that stared at us from – I'd say – a distance of some eighteen metres. Even from a distance of eighteen metres, we could hear its heavy breathing. For the first time, I believed that the tapes given to me by Kevin Stubbs, supposedly of a gigantopithecus breathing in a copse on Chipstead Downs, were not of the Dave Bowman character during the 'Deactivation of Hal9000' scene from the popular science fiction film *2001: A Space Odyssey*, recorded from a television. I felt that the world was slowly revolving behind me, like a giant wheel, and soon I would be suspended by the soles of my boots with the sky below.

I must have been the last of us to realise that something had kicked off up in the trees. When The DJ went white it crossed my mind that this might be a bluff, a feint so he could have another crack at The Funnel's soft under-particles.

I checked back.

The Funnel was on his hands and knees, head bowed.

This is why I didn't realise at first that it wasn't only The DJ who had gone white.

Sci-Borg: she was squinting as if the sun had come over the horizon in a desert.

She took a step backwards, almost losing her footing.

She pressed her palms to her cheeks.

And then I looked up.

There.

In the woods.

In the gap in the trees.

In the dusk.

In the air tonight.

Bristling.

Rampant.

Erect.

Indifferent.

Inhuman.

Serene.

Gigantic.

Gigantopithecus.
Gigantopithecus, ROAR.

> • ⟨

First off, it's like a kick in the bollocks. You feel like your hair has fallen out in one go. You think you're going to chuck up. You're in one of those dreams where you're standing in your childhood bedroom spitting your teeth into your palm. Your jaw hangs so low it tears at the joints and tugs at the back of your skull.

Then come the tremors, the tingles that flow up your arms and jangle your scalp. You're vibrating. Your eyes can't take it all in. It's so huge, not just in person but the implication of it.

There's something having a breakdown in your guts now. It's begging you to turn tail, to run, back to the safety of your car, your town, to your makeshift shelter at the end of a cul-de-sac that only exists because for the last four thousand years they have allowed us mastery of the open spaces.

This is the fear, the 'shatting-up effect'. You've got to ride it. You mustn't swerve. You must KNOW. You must give in to the EVIDENCE OF YOUR OWN EYES, and when you do, the modern world and its endless boredom where nothing magical happens, and the being passed over, kept indoors and left behind and not believed will fall away. You will be carried into the forests of our forefathers.

I had been waiting for this moment for all my life. I rode the fear. I was King of the Woods, Partisan of Romance, the Knower. I had done it. Finally, I had got one over on all of Science, Science itself, all of its layers and the levels of management and red tape they put there to hedge you into your cramped little pod, your Post-It-sized life, the misplaced password that is your life, where you know your place, where you're happy just paying off your loans and believing the lies as you breed and you die without ever standing anywhere near to the precipice of greatness, without ever getting close to the FACTS.

On the Common, I was almost jealous of Maxine. Her mind was getting a proper diagnostic now. It was being rebooted, returned to its factory setting. Her consciousness was downloading God's upgrade. The first time is like realising that milk is really black, or the Sun orbits the Earth, or aliens from another dimension did come here thousands of years ago to build landing strips in the Nazca Desert.

From now on she was going to have to see everything with the evidence of her own eyes. The truth was growing more powerful and more soulful with every second she stood there gawping at the Long Man.

Gorgo was right. He's always light years ahead of the rest of us. She would be the poster girl for the GIT. She would be the cheerleader of the revolution that's coming to the world. Like it or not, she and I were bonded in perpetuity. Like Adam and Eve, we didn't ask to be shoved together in the Garden, but meddlesome and cosmic matchmakers made us talk to each other, and wary as we may have been, we sort of get on so we might as well make a night of it.

Up on the ridge, Giganto cocked his head. Something clicked inside my brain. For a second I seemed to see Maxine and me as if I was outside of myself, dangling from a bungee rope attached to a cloud.

From here, all was bright sunshine. Rose petals drifted across the Common. I could smell cinnamon and something like those long thin sticks hippies burn that make you feel a bit sick. The grass was the greenest of grasses and the trees the tallest of trees. We were high up the slope. We were naked. She was wearing a headdress of daisies. We were hand in hand. The gigantopithecus was before us, gigantic, hairy and with a cone-shaped head. In unison we fell to our knees before it. Petals swirled around us, and the deer and the badgers emerged from the woods and lined up on either side of us. We were getting married, and we didn't even invite The Funnel or The DJ. It was just Nature and us. The gigantopithecus unleashed a mighty howl that echoed through Andreasweald. Clouds parted. Pollen rose. Fronds rustled. Dead leaves fluttered up from the ground. Rabbits leapt for their warrens and the squirrels jumped from branch to branch, and out there in the depths of the forest other howls are returned to us as we are joined together in eternity by eternity itself.

I blinked.

The wedding scene vanished.

Giganto had not moved. He was still up there. The Funnel was chanting in a foreign language behind us. The DJ's teeth chattered. A sweaty heat radiated from Maxine.

I was cool, though. I was calm. I was staring right into its red glowing eyes and holding my stare like I've practised in the mirror for ten thousand hours.

I was about to raise the camcorder. I was about to *record*. Giganto wasn't spooked. He wasn't going anywhere as long as we kept still. All I had to do was hold the kit steady and in a matter of days, everything would be different.

These images would hit the front pages.

We would be on the news and all over the Internet, all over the world.

The truth would be out.

No one would go to work.

Everyone would call in sick.

Everyone would sit still and think.

All the blokes in The Churn would weep into their hands.

Gorgo Gartree would punch the air.

He would shout, 'Bung it all on, MonkeyMagic,' and then lay a wreath on the grave of Jackie Hogg.

My face would be on every hoarding, on the front page of every newspaper and home page of every website. I would be on chat shows. I would write books and have books written about me. There would be photographs of me on the dust jackets of hardbacks. I would be on the cover of the *Daily Mail*. There would be documentaries and films about this moment. There would be action figures and my own branded range of thermal imaging cameras and night-vision goggles. The cash would flow in. I would have to get an accountant, and a secretary, and someone to do my laundry, probably. Maybe I'd need a body double, because science fundamentalists would put a hit out on me.

I'd be fighting off Giganto groupies, too. All the girls would want a swing through the trees with MonkeyMagic. But I'd be married to Maxine now, for my crimes, so she'd have to be nice to me and trust me.

Nature programmes on the BBC would be presented by me. I'd be sent on adventures, all around the world. The man who proved the existence of the North Surrey

Gigantopithecus would be sent to prove them all, all the ape-like bipeds of the world, all the rectal hominids: yeti, alma, sasquatch, orang pendek, the Grey Man of Ben MacDhui, yowie, kapre and batutut. I would tick them all off.

The North Surrey Gigantopithecus is us, you see; us, you and me. FACT.

It tells us where we've come from. It shows us what we have lost. It's the last piece of the evolutionary jigsaw, the final link in a snapped chain. From this moment on, we will know who we are meant to be.

It was the last part of me, too, the bit that was stolen from Kevin Stubbs, the ape-shaped man, the man-shaped ape, the lost moments of my time, the key to my life. My life, that will now make perfect sense.

When this got out, when this hit the newsstands and the search engines, everyone in the world was going to become a Kevin Stubbs.

Everyone's Kevin now.

Everyone's MonkeyMagic.

FACT.

And Kyrylo.

Kyrylo and I.

My boy.

My son.

Inheritor of Wonders.

Prince of the World.

My gift to humanity.

I'd told you the truth.

I let you in on it from the start.

We would be reunited.

We would be together in the forests of the Earth.

> • <

I lifted the camcorder. The gigantopithecus was in my sights now, in the crosshairs of the viewfinder: gigantic, hairy and with a very cone-shaped bonce.

I had my finger on the trigger.

GIGANTOPITHECUS INTELLIGENCE TEAM

REPORT #214 (CATEGORY A)

SECTION 7

Report on Field Trip II/ (x)

At this point, I realised that the witness had fled. GIT Cryptozoologist Funnel was still prostrated on the ground. I must admit that in this moment I felt unprepared and unable to provide sufficient leadership to the GIT, and sought the advice of Secondary Investigator Stubbs, who had, I now conceded, far more experience of close encounters with the gigantopithecus. I tried to keep resolutely still so as not to frighten the creature. I whispered to Secondary Investigator Stubbs that he needed to switch on his camcorder and film the monster. When he asked me to be quiet, I whispered to him that I needed his advice on how to behave now that the creature was in our sights, that we had evidence and proof if only we could film it steadily. Secondary Investigator Stubbs put his arm across my chest and again asked me to stay silent. At this point he crouched down and placed the camcorder on the grass.

Notice the way she changes her tune at this point in Report #214. It's no longer the 'cryptid'. It's not a 'rectal hominid' or a 'large primate'. It's 'the creature', 'the monster', like she's suddenly found herself in a horror film. There's nothing like a Category A encounter with a gigantopithecus to reboot anyone's hard drive.

Anyway, this part of Maxine's report is also more or less true. She is right about The DJ, too. He'd shat himself. The thumps of his trainers receded as he bricked it back towards the van.

I expected The Funnel would stop reciting now and join us in this moment of communion. He stayed where he was, though. This is why I would never advise anyone to take up yoga. You miss things.

Compared to those two, I have to hand it to Maxine: she showed some conkers. She didn't pants herself or anything. Even so, I was getting worried. It's hard, the first time. She was shaking. She was about to scream, or worse. I didn't want to hear this. I didn't want to see her get upset. She was my wife now. It was written in a vision. I might not like what was written in the vision, but ancients had written it. I had to put up with it, too. I had to be loyal. It was like one of those dynastic marriages in the time of kings and queens, the joining of two houses, the marriage of Science and Knowing.

It was here that she said, 'Oh dear. Dear me. It's there. It's there, Kevin, the thing. It's horrible. I don't know what to do.'

'Look at him, he's majestic. Gigantic.'

'You were right all along. Switch on the camera. Film it.'

'Hush, my darling.'

'People have to know about this. People have to see it.'

I'm not saying that just for an instant here I didn't get a lot of pleasure out of these words coming out of her sushi-hole. I'm also not saying that I didn't love all this. There he was, ahead of us, the Long Man, the Missing Link. Not another shadow behind a greenhouse, or a smudged, maybe-footprint on a building site in Tooting Graveney, but the North Surrey Gigantopithecus: erect, rampant, serenely indifferent.

The way she'd said it, though. Something in her voice: 'people have to know about this, people have to see it'.

Any second, these feelings of victory would fade. I would stop revelling in this day of days and pull the trigger. I would capture sustained, stable, in-focus, verifiable and unhoaxable footage of the North Surrey Gigantopithecus.

But I wasn't alone, was I? Maxine was here. Gorgo had brought her in so that people would believe us when this happened. People don't want to believe anything reported by stone Knowers like The Funnel and me. They'll only believe it if it comes from someone like her, with letters after her name and a respectable and glamorous-sounding job like science teacher, who hasn't been chucked out of a pub for being slapped by a woman after a Hominid Rex gig, or deported from the Democratic Republic of Congo for asking too many questions about lost dinosaurs. Maxine was going to be the face of this. She was – fair enough – going to have to do the talking. In front of the TV cameras I'd probably start swearing, and The Funnel might talk a load of sex-magick bollocks that no one's ever going to be ready for.

And then what would happen?

She wasn't going to be able to stop them. All the Science lot she knows were going to be scouring this manor with helicopters and troop carriers. There would be armies of government goon squads with tasers and tranquilizer dart guns. They were going to flush him out. If they didn't kill him and have him stuffed and stuck in a science museum, they'd stick him in a miserable zoo. Kids like The DJ's would come and chuck Kit-Kats at him. They wouldn't care that he only liked bagels and Sunpat Crunchy. Men like the men from The Churn would try and get him pissed so he showed his arse and mouthed off, like I once saw them do to a chimpanzee in a zoo in Lloret del Mar in Spain.

At the old Chessington Zoo, when I was kid, before it became a funfair, there were these great white pens where a slope led down to a pool of grimy water. The polar bear paced slowly around all day, snout to the ground, sniffing for something that wasn't there, his small brain ticking with visions of the Arctic and dreams of going through someone's bins in Manitoba.

'Kevin,' said Maxine. 'Do you think we need the Heat Ray?'

Heat Ray? She was even speaking our lingo now, the language of GIT.

I put my arm across her chest.

'It's a great bit of kit, love, but not now. Hush.'

It was here that I crouched down and rested the camcorder on the dirt.

GIGANTOPITHECUS INTELLIGENCE TEAM

REPORT #214 (CATEGORY A)

SECTION 7

<u>Report on Field Trip II/ (xi)</u>

Secondary Investigator Stubbs held still, as if deep in thought, and raised his hands and cupped them to his mouth. He made a noise, then started to sprint towards the woods, wailing and waving his arms. In the process, he scared the gigantopithecus, which in turn disappeared into the trees and headed in the direction of the golf course.

Too right I made a noise.

First off, though, I got rid of the rest of the kit. I chucked away the wraparound aviator shades. They made me not only *look* stupid but *think* stupid.

I threw off the Sci-Bionic Parabolic Microphone and Short Range Listening Device, aka the Sonic Scream, the one I'd meanly kept running after Maxine's mobile rang while we were doing ops on Wilderness Island in Carshalton and some pupil had got hold of her number and rang up to call her a minge.

I tossed the night-vision goggles over my shoulder, the ones I'd been wearing when I said I'd seen the Nonsuch Kong, when I probably had only seen some shadows.

I dropped my iPhone, the one I'd used to post the Banstead Bigfoot Footage on YouTube to drop The DJ right in it.

I placed the two-grand's worth of thermal imaging camera, aka the Heat Ray, alongside the camcorder, the very same one I'd bought when Bohuslava wanted me to use the money to pay for her mother's cataract operation.

I got shot of the plaster of Paris kit that, on the night Kyrylo was born, I was using to take casts of outsized footprints on a muddy track over at Beddington Sewage Works.

I dumped the scat jars that Bohuslava had thrown back at me after I'd given them to Kyrylo for this seventh birthday.

I shrugged off my laptop bag, let it fall to the ground, the one I'd used to watch Bigfoot videos on YouTube and once accidently clicked on a popup saying Meet Ukrainian Brides Now.

I may have made some dodgy moves in my life.

I may have made some bad calls and ordered my wife like a pizza and been a little overbearing to some women and gigantopithecus deniers because they disagreed with me, but now I was going to make it all better.

I would do a good, great thing for once in my life.

I raised my hands and cupped my palms.

I sucked in as much air as I could, drew it into my gut.

I took a last look at it: gigantic, hairy.

Then I let off the howl of howls.

Ahaaaarrraaararaaaaaaaaa aaaaaaaaaaaaaaaaaaaaaaaaa aaaaaaaaaaaahhhhhhhh-ah

It didn't move at first. It kept where it was, its arms dangling at its sides, head cocked, red eye-shine. I'd screwed up the howl of howls as well. The big, friendly lump was going to howl back, not freak and scarper. Maxine would have time to scoop up the camcorder and shoot him herself.

I ripped off my T-shirt, tightened my stomach muscles, breathed in, breathed out, sprang forward on the balls of my feet and pelted up the slope.

Giganto shivered, shook, stepped back inside the treeline and started his majestic lope.

I kept running, working my elbows like pistons, jaw locked. I knew what would happen now. What happened here could not be kept quiet. The Funnel had seen Giganto. He wouldn't keep schtum. Only a highly specialist and niche audience (aka me) would believe The Funnel, but Maxine had seen it too, and so had The DJ. News of the sighting would leak. There would be reports, eyewitness accounts and forum discussions. Investigators from ManBeast GB and Knowers from the *Daily Mail* would come up here to claim a piece of it. All the talk would be: MonkeyMagic had it in his sights. If it was right there, why didn't he film it? Why didn't he solve, once and for all, the greatest mystery of all time, the existence of the North Surrey Gigantopithecus, the Missing Link, the Secret of Life? We always knew MonkeyMagic was a psycho and a fanatic. Now we know he's a hoaxer as well.

A dirty hoaxer.

Kevin Stubbs is a hoaxer.

Kevin Stubbs will forever be The Man who Hoaxed the North Surrey Gigantopithecus, the subject of a one-off documentary on some lame YouTube channel no one subscribes to.

In the trees now, momentum carried me further than I'd wanted. At first I couldn't see it. He was there, though, shoulders wide, fur rippling as he headed for the golf course. They were going to say I was a hoaxer. I was prepared for that. I was resigned. I wanted a last look at it. I picked up the pace again, into the trees.

The thing is, it's supposed to be fast, with its huge strides and super-ape-like biped muscles, but as I puffed along the track I was gaining on it, and as I gained on it and closed the gap, it wasn't that big. It was a baby one after all. That's what I thought at first, until I heard its breathing. It wasn't so much breathing as wheezing. It was sick, then. It must be suffering with gut-ache. Maybe it had eaten something that The DJ's mates had left behind at the site of the barbecue, some disco biscuits or Hawaiian pizza.

It was now silhouetted in the glow of the streetlamps of the A217, aka the Brighton Road, that separates the Common from the golf course.

I was so close to it, and it really wasn't that much bigger than me, if it was bigger than me at all. I reached out my hand. My fingers brushed its fur. It turned its head and with a desperate spurt of effort it pulled away from me.

I stopped.

Panting.

A sound that was a rushing in my ears – the blood throbbing at my temples, I thought – was no such thing.

I glanced through the trees, up towards the road.

Headlights swept through the trunks like a UFO sighting.

The whoosh of an accelerating car.

The gigantopithecus was still running.

I held out my hand as if I could reach out and pull him back by the scruff.

'No, mate, no. Please. Stop.'

GIGANTOPITHECUS INTELLIGENCE TEAM

REPORT #214 (CATEGORY A)

SECTION 7

<u>Report on Field Trip II/ (xii)</u>

By the time I reached the trees, I could see neither the gigantopithecus nor Secondary Investigator Stubbs. I followed in their general direction. After two or three minutes, some way in the distance I heard a screech of brakes and a loud thump. There followed the sound of a car door slamming and a barrage of coarse Anglo-Saxon phrases.

Exiting the trees, I now emerged onto a grassy strip alongside the A217 Brighton Road. Ahead of me, a large black 4x4 vehicle fitted with a bull bar and UV under-lighting was paused on the road with its engine still running. The gigantopithecus was laid out on the road behind it. A bare-chested, overweight, middle-aged man in tracksuit bottoms and a baseball cap was kicking it. He shouted repeatedly that the gigantopithecus was 'worse than Savile'.

To their left, Secondary Investigator Stubbs had adopted the position of someone sitting on an invisible chair or showing off an invisible motorcycle. He emitted a scream. This was emitted protractedly in the style of the 'Giganto Howl' he deploys to attract the cryptid on nocturnal field trips.

Yes, when she pitched up I did scream. I'll put my hand up to that.

I did not, however, scream in the style of the Giganto Howl.

The Giganto Howl is: *Ahaaaarrraaararaaaaaaaaaaaaaa aaaaaaaaaaaaaaaaaahhhhhhhh-hah.*

This scream was more: *Naaaaaaaaargg-NO! Noahhhhhhhhhhhhhhhhh.*

Other than that, I'm nit-picking here. Must be habit.

From my place in the woods I'd watched the gigantopithecus run headlong into the road, despite the onrushing lights and the engine buzz of what I could tell was a pretty massive bit of kit. It sounded like one of those 4x4s that I've always fancied owning myself, so I could fortify it and fight road wars on the former M25 after civilisation breaks down and it all kicks off in Sutton.

If the gigantopithecus had been fully grown and mature, and if it wasn't sick with some cardiovascular illness it had contracted after scavenging from the remains of The DJ's barbecue, it would, cool as you like, have paused in the road, reached down using its Ninja of the Blackness skills, gripped the bull bar and hoisted the 4x4 over its cone-shaped. In doing so, it would only have added to its legend.

But the gigantopithecus was immature, skittish.

I'd shat it up.

It didn't even see the car.

A soft thump.

A blur flew back over the roof of the car.

It landed on the road.

Screech of brakes.

This baseball-cap knob with no top on – Sutton down to his balls – leapt from the now stationary car. As I made it to the verge, he'd reached the body. Rather than help the poor thing he started to kick it.

'Paedo… come round 'ere for our fuckin' kids, you nonce.'

When I caught up, all that was in my head was to do over this outsized, worm-brained, hominid-shaped manifestation of the Red Darkness of Sutton made flesh. I'd have to take him down quick. Otherwise the filth would arrive and two huge bare-chested blokes from Sutton would be slugging it out on the road in front of clear Category A evidence of the North Surrey Gigantopithecus, aka the corpse of the Banstead Bigfoot. I needed to get the gentle gigantopithecus buried in the woods before anyone else got here.

The hair around its head was all matted with blood and the blood had leaked out all over the road. Its calves jerked up and down as each kick landed. The Red Darkness man couldn't get enough of the kicking. He kicked it in the hip and the ribs and the shoulder. He kicked it in the face. His kicks became slower, more precise and hard. He must have realised that the monster on the tarmac wasn't going to fight back, that it was down, in its place, that its days of lurking and brooding on the hideous acts it had planned for his hideous offspring were over, that he'd won again, added another drinking story to his legend, another glorious triumph to his saga.

He still kept kicking, though, even when the head started to shudder.

This close, the fur on its head was a much darker brown to the lighter, tawny fur on its shoulders. The fur on its head swept down to a noticeably straight hem, and there was now a gap between that hem and the darker fur of his back, and each time a kick struck home, the hem slapped against the fur around his shoulders. A zip ran all along his spine. His arse didn't have buttocks or a crack. His foot had been ripped clean off by the accident.

Specks of green light widened in the distance, the glint of Maxine's night-vision goggles as she sprinted from the treeline.

She said, 'Stop it, you animal, he's dead. Can't you see that? He's dead.'

She held a hairy foot in her hand.

I screamed.

I'm not ashamed.

No one would have heard, apart from Maxine, and maybe, if he could hear anything at all, the man with the kicks.

GIGANTOPITHECUS INTELLIGENCE TEAM

REPORT #214 (CATEGORY A)

SECTION 7

<u>Report on Field Trip II/ (xiii)</u>

When I reached the scene, I saw blood on the road. At first, I thought that one of the creature's feet had been severed by the collision. On inspection, the foot turned out to be a large carpet slipper in the shape of a gorilla's foot. As I approached it became discernible that the creature's fur was synthetic.

I requested that the man in the baseball cap desist from kicking the creature. It was only later that the identity of the man in the baseball cap was revealed as co-witness Donny 'One Punch' Dawkers, who had been summoned by the witness to collect him from a nearby car park. After negotiation, Donny 'One Punch' Dawkers agreed to stop kicking the subject and attributing paraphiliae to the subject without objective or first-hand oral evidence. At this point, Cryptozoologist Derek Funnel rejoined us.

Secondary Investigator Stubbs, Cryptozoologist Derek Funnel and myself then rolled the creature over. We discovered that the head was in fact a mask of the popular 'Chewbacca' character from the *Star Wars* series of children's films, a large, bipedal hominid with only a rudimentary capacity for speech, but somehow the ability to manipulate advanced technology and who allegedly originates from another world. A mask of this type is readily available to purchase at the U Krazee Kidz party and novelty store in the Times Square Shopping Centre in nearby Sutton. Red Christmas lights had been attached either side of the eye sockets. They were connected by a flex to a switch that lay in the palm of the subject's limp paw.

I removed the mask. Beneath the mask, it was revealed to the GIT and Donny 'One Punch' Dawkers that former GIT Lead Investigator and Founder Edward Gartree, prior to his death on the Brighton Road at approximately 21.45, had been wearing the suit.

She did take off the mask, I have to give this to her. Notice, though, that she doesn't know that Chewbacca is a Wookiee. The Funnel probably believes in Wookiees, but even if they are real, I knew that the North Surrey Gigantopithecus could be many things but not a Wookiee.

Crouching, Maxine wiped the blood from the emerging face with her hand. I dipped down to join her, at this moment hoping against hope that whoever had been inside that suit was still, by some miracle, alive.

She put her bloody hand on my shoulder.

'Don't look, Kevin,' she said.

Too late.

My eyes shrivelled. My gut hollowed.

That face I'd first seen on TV, speaking into a microphone on the night after the Sutton Cock sighting. The charisma and dignity of that man. King of the Knowers. The man who started it all. Founder. Visionary. The original. The closest thing I'd ever had to a father. The closest thing I ever had to Arthur C. Dad. The man who had provided a model for me on how to be a father myself. The man who showed me the way of the woods and the way of the kit. The legend. The man who told me earlier today that I would be a legend, too. The only man I'd ever believed in.

As if by magic, The Funnel appeared.

'Oh my,' he said. 'This is neither fish nor fowl, my friends.'

Donny 'One-Punch' Dawkers loomed on the other side of the body, his shoulders wide, his chin sunk into his chest, no frown, no grimace, no smile, nothing, a great fleshy letter H standing erect on the tarmac.

'All your nonsense,' said Maxine, 'and now someone has been killed.'

I'm not sure if she said this to me or to Dawkers.

She might have said it to Eddie.

Blue flashes behind us reflected off the trees on either side of the road. Tall shadows, humanoid, emerged from the lights.

I raised my arms in surrender, put my hands on either side of my head. I looked up and waited for the whir of rotor blades. Instructions barked through a megaphone. Rough stuff. Gunpoint. I did not know where they would take us. We had not prepared a story for this sort of thing, at least not since Maxine became Lead Investigator. I readied myself for the blows.

Out of the shimmer, two tiny policewomen in soft caps walked towards us.

GIGANTOPITHECUS INTELLIGENCE TEAM

REPORT #214 (CATEGORY A)

SECTION 8

<u>CONCLUSION</u>:

The 6 July 'Banstead Bigfoot' footage is a certifiable hoax.

Furthermore, given the similarity of the Gartree-Chewbacca costume – after all photographs and footage from during my time as Lead Investigator were analysed again as preliminary research for Report #214 – it is highly likely that all of these cases were also, as I had suspected, hoaxes perpetrated by Gartree for reasons unknown.

Given former GIT Lead Investigator and Founder Edward Gartree's involvement in these recent hoaxes, it can only be surmised that all cases investigated by the GIT since 1988 were also hoaxes perpetrated on the more vulnerable, less psychologically sophisticated members of the GIT by Edward Gartree and, until his death, Jack Hogg.

I have found no evidence for a large bipedal hominid living secretly in the London Borough of Sutton and its surrounding environs, forests and arable farmland.

I resign my position as GIT Lead Investigator forthwith, and strongly recommend that the project be disbanded.

It wasn't until the night before the funeral that I went looking for the film. Not the so-called 'Banstead Bigfoot' film. That was a certifiable and poxy hoax. I never wanted to see that ever again. I was after *the* film, the film that started it all, the Gartree-Hogg/Sutton Cock Footage.

I had the film on a VHS tape somewhere. Eddie Gartree had given me that tape. It was an original copy. I wanted to see it as it was meant to be seen: grainy, flickering, jerky and in and out of focus. I wanted to see it one last time before I said goodbye.

I hadn't seen any TV since the accident. I hadn't left the flat or been to work. I told iiSkipper that my dad had died. I was taking it bad, wouldn't be in for a while. I'd have been useless if I'd gone into work anyway. I'd have been slipping things and breaking things and bursting into tears in front of Clive and that Becca. I was going through something that I knew I had to go through.

Up until now I had left GIT matters alone. I hadn't looked at the news or the web forums. I knew what they would all be saying. Sos_the_Rope, NatterJacqui and Man_in_a_Suit would be spluttering up their Chablis because the Man who Started It All, Eddie Gartree, had been exposed as a hoaxer and flattened in front of his idiot-minion MonkeyMagic. All the newspapers, even the *Daily Mail,* would have made a connection between the contested Gartree-Hogg footage and the obvious and poxy hoax footage of the Banstead Bigfoot. I could feel the messages and posts humming in the air. If I was in the lounge, I could feel them pulse in the kitchen. If I was in the bathroom, I could sense them swirling in the hall, like that ectoplasm stuff The Funnel says is real.

The phone kept ringing. I didn't answer the phone.

I knew who was ringing. One of them always hung up after four rings, and the other would let it ring on and on and on before she hung up, then call again exactly two minutes later.

The knocks on the door started.

First, he came. It was the middle of the night. I watched him from behind my bedroom curtains. He waited on the garden path, draped in a hooded black smock and swinging a little chain around his ring finger.

She came in the daytime, late afternoons. I didn't let her in. I wouldn't have known what to say if I had.

They came together once.

They both called my name.

Eventually, she posted a note through the door with kind words written on it and details about the funeral.

I spent most of my time in bed.

Sometimes I moved to the sofa.

I got used to the sense that somewhere else I was the centre of attention. Some of that attention was well-meant concern. Some of it was laughter at my expense.

I did play with the idea of starting a new research group on my own. I even came up with a name, but it all seemed trivial now. Trivial, naff and deadly.

When I closed my eyes, I was always on that path between the trees.

I can almost grab his shoulder and pull him to the ground.

I stop and pant and shout helplessly as he blunders into the road.

On the road, One-Punch is working Eddie over.

Eddie is dead again.

It is dead.

When I opened my eyes, I was made of slush.

When I tried to sleep, her calm, dignified voice would come back to me.

Can't you see that he's dead?

Only she understood what was really going on here. Unlike Dawkers and me, she was speaking about, not through the Red Darkness that for years we had allowed to control us. She wasn't one of the angry, blinkered men of Sutton who never had a chance to be anything different.

Dawkers would do time.

He would go down for this.

I was going down, too, but there would be a different judge and jury.

> • <

Sat on the floor, in front of the TV, I played the tape. Part of me still hoped it would inspire the same expansion of my mind it had all those years ago and I would be able to piece together an alibi for Gorgo. There had to have been method here, and a purpose. All those years of GIT Supreme and our friendship couldn't have been founded on a lie. Gorgo would not have lied to me. He couldn't have been hoaxing me from the beginning. Maybe he hoaxed only on the night that he died. Or if he had hoaxed the 6 July footage, he might have been winding up Maxine (fair enough). Or he was trying to inspire some particularly useless kids (The DJ's kids and his mates' kids) into taking a new direction in life, giving them a higher calling, something to belong to, just like he had me. Or he was simply desperate. He'd rigged the game because was getting on, getting old, getting ready to quit the field. Before he went to the Great Squatch Hunt in the Sky, he wanted to leave a sign that would inspire a whole new generation. The Banstead Bigfoot Film was a legacy hoax. It was for a good cause.

It was still possible that the original Gartree-Hogg/Sutton Cock Footage was not a hoax. FACT.

The flickery first fifteen seconds of the footage again shuddered me into a different, more exciting world. As Gorgo tries to level and point the lens, a tubing effect smears from a street light and strobes a moving blotch in the glimmer.

This is as good as anything produced by the Yanks.

All you can hear is Gorgo's voice: 'What's that? Who is that?'

On the other side of the crossroads now you can clearly see a gigantopithecus pause in front of the window of Knobs and Knockers. The Subject has its back to us. It's gigantic, hairy, with long swinging arms and a cone-shaped head. It's a dirty great gigantopithecus, if you're a Knower.

However, now that I look at it with all the idealism kicked out of me by real life in its most brutal form, I take Maxine's point that you can't really tell how tall it is, even if you can discount that the cameraman was skilled in the production of visual effects and could have been having a right laugh. Funny how I didn't notice that before.

Then the Subject turns and you see its glowing red eyes.

Now, I've had some booze-induced headcrackers in the

past, and I've spent all night crapping myself in the woods with all sorts kicking off, and I've never had red-eye as bad as that.

This is the moment that got to Jackie Hogg, where he experienced the 'shatting-up effect'.

Something occurs to me now, though. You don't hear this on the tape. You don't see him fall to his knees.

This might have a logical explanation. Gorgo is filming a dirty great rectal hominid and doesn't want to pan the camera to his mate who is going mental on the pavement. Nor do you hear any cry or whimper from Jackie Hogg. The audio is muffled, true, and he might have been struck dumb.

I was struck dumb in Morden Crematorium, my first time.

The DJ and Maxine were struck dumb on Banstead Common.

On the other hand, Maxine's counter-theory has always been that Jackie is not behind Gorgo at all. Maxine has speculated that in front of Knobs and Knockers, that's Jackie prancing about in a bear suit.

Her cited evidence is that, according to her research, Jackie Hogg had never been a paratrooper and was in fact a well-known costumier who worked on several ropey science fiction series and annoying, puppet-based kids programmes in the seventies. It's rumoured that he designed the original 'Bungle Bear' suit for some weird and unsettling kids show called *Rainbow*, that I didn't know about because it was obviously inappropriate when I was growing up in The Church of the Poisoned Mind. Apparently, the first Bungle suit was too scary for little kids, too like a real bear, and had to be replaced with the softer-looking teddy-like costume that most people now, it would seem, associate with Bungle.

I am now entertaining this conjecture as a possible theory.

Then you get the lope. Due to the height of the gigantopithecus, Gorgo struggles with the camera and the lens zigzags as the beast wanders across the road. Arm-swing is clearly visible. The cone-shaped appears in profile. The Subject realises it's being observed, so it picks up speed. It vanishes into the alley that led to Carats nightclub.

I rewound the tape and paused it just before the gigantopithecus turns.

I watched the turn and the lope again, then again and again.

Could this be someone in a bear suit, the original Bungle costume too scary for little kids, or some customized version of it (extended arms, clown shoes, smallish dunce's cap stuck inside the mask to impersonate a cone-shaped, fairy lights for eyes, etc.)? Or could it still be a majestic creature out of time?

I couldn't tell. It's too blotchy, too shaky. It doesn't stay still.

All I can say is that it does look very much like what we see on the 6 July footage. The profile, though, when it crosses the road towards the alley, doesn't look like Chewbacca, aka a Wookiee. Is it more likely to be a gigantopithecus, then? Or, had the original Bungle head perished or gone bald, and Eddie had to buy a new mask when Jackie was no longer around to make one? The Bungle head would have been a unique, bespoke bit of kit, so Jackie would have had to settle for a Wookiee for the 6 July hoax.

I turned off the tape. I tried to process all the times we went out into the woods, and all the times we investigated a sighting.

I couldn't remember a time in the early days when I'd seen it with Gorgo and Jackie *both* present.

Is it significant that after Jackie died I never saw the gigantopithecus with Gorgo alongside me?

I am not saying that there can't be a gigantopithecus in Sutton.

I am saying that Jackie and Gorgo may have, after all, hoaxed at Sutton Cock (Maxine says the date is a clue – filmed 31 March, broadcast 1 April – but I think that's a coincidence). Twenty-five years later, Gorgo, alone this time, hoaxed the 6 July and subsequent sighting.

You can't argue with the latter.

That's about the only thing I know for sure now.

> • <

On top of all this, Boho had been phoning me. Letting a phone ring until Doomsday is her MO.

This meant that Maxine must have spoken to Boho already.

Boho knew that Eddie Gartree was dead and that Eddie was the North Surrey Gigantopithecus.

Soon I would be dragged to some cackhole, like the Chicago Rock. I'd have to swallow my pride and agree with Boho that there are no big monkeys in Sutton if I wanted to mend some fences with Kyrylo. I have been the victim of a big monkey hoax, but we can put it behind us and get on with being one big monkey family if I can apologize for the long absences, the inappropriate birthday presents, the shouting and accidently – I swear – abandoning him in a van in the middle of the night while I went stalking shadows.

I was not sure what was out there now.

Out there in the hills and the woodland.

I had been hoaxed.

> • <

I'll put my hands up and admit that I thought long and hard about whether or not to go to Gorgo's funeral. It wasn't that the hoax had killed all the respect I had for the man. There were still good times to remember, great days, moments where there was something in the woods that we couldn't explain. And I'd been there when he died.

I had seen the man die. This meant something, hoaxer or not.

But I had no wheels. God knows where the van was now. I'd left it at the Common. The service would be held in Morden. I had to travel there under my own speed. When I left the house, no crowd of journalists and photographers waited for me. No one buttonholed me at the bus stop. No one even sat next to me on the bus. No press pack swarmed around the crematorium gates.

At the chapel doors, old people stood in groups under the portico, relatives of Eddie Gartree, I supposed. I dreaded seeing them, but The Funnel and Maxine hadn't arrived yet.

I found myself wandering around in little circles at the side of the chapel, trying to come up with some good memories of Eddie Gartree. It wasn't that I didn't have any. Out of the flat now, back in the world, it preoccupied me that I hadn't been chased down the roads by the press, reptilian freemasons, or friends of Donny 'One Punch' Dawkers trying to persuade me not to testify against him in the age-old north Surrey fashion. From the top deck of the bus, the concrete had looked simply grey. The trees were trees. The parks were parks. The people were people going about their daily business of wearing baseball caps back-to-front and disappointing pensioners. Morden was just another place, a cemetery at the end of the Northern Line.

Of course, there is more to Morden than the cemetery. There's a KFC, for a start, but as more mourners pitched up I remembered that I had stood in this graveyard with Gorgo on another occasion, except he'd been alive.

> • <

The moon had been full and high over Morden. Gorgo and I were crouched down behind a white marble headstone, dressed in black, burnt cork smeared across our faces, eyes trained on a line of weeping willows that fluttered in the breeze.

Earlier, Gorgo had rung me to ask for my help. He'd read the letter I'd sent him after the Sutton Cock footage aired, and he'd been impressed by my belief and enthusiasm. Someone had reported a sighting of the 'NSG', as he called it then (aka the North Surrey Gigantopithecus that had been terrorizing the manor since the Sutton Cock encounter). An old dear laying a wreath had seen a large ape-like biped standing among the headstones. Mr Hogg was unavailable. Would I ride shotgun on this expedition?

I was so happy. I belonged to the Knowers.

If you were a Knower and attuned to these things, there was Category B evidence all over that site: floral tributes had been kicked about and were strewn over the gravel paths (later, The Funnel would explain to me that the gigantopithecus is immortal and takes any opportunity, the world over, to jeer at death and our rituals of remembrance). We found a weird blotchy print in some gravel and what looked like white dog muck all over the place. They had changed the dog food recipes by then, so whatever had done its business here was unlikely to have been a dog.

Gorgo and I had carried out an expert reconnaissance of the site. As we wandered around the trees and the long gravel paths, he showed me a few tricks and techniques that I still use today. I learned how to bang a tree with a thick stick to provoke a reply. Oh yeah, and we only went and got one, didn't we. I smashed the shit out of this tree with a big stick and five seconds later, off in the distance: *KER-WRACK*.

'It's here,' said Gorgo, 'it's close.'

Then he showed me how to do the call. He yowled at the moon, varying his pitch from a baboon-like scream to a tailing hiss. After that, I told him that I was now experiencing the 'shatting-up effect'. Even if monsters did not exist, we were in the middle of a graveyard in the middle of the night, in Morden.

We retreated to a vantage point at the centre of the cemetery. Here, we could keep an eye on the trees and have clear exit routes if the Lurker in the Willows turned out to be a cornered and none-too-friendly nine-foot, bipedal ape creature with red glowing eyes.

Around 3 a.m., we both saw a figure in the trees, gigantic and hairy, with long, swinging arms and distinctive cone-shaped cranium. Its silhouette lurched into a shaft of moonlight. Then it loped briefly along the treeline, until it vanished into cover.

> • <

Standing there, though, looking out over that very site, I couldn't help thinking that I'd be a spanner if I didn't entertain the possibility that Gorgo had played an elaborate practical joke on me that night. It was Jackie who had messed up the floral tributes and left the footprint and done things to his dog's food so it would shat white dog muck he could plant all over the site, and it was Jackie who had returned the wood knock. The figure we saw in the trees, barely discernible in the darkness, was Jackie in the original Bungle Bear costume that was too scary for little kids. It wasn't just any old practical joke. It was one designed for my benefit alone, constructed entirely at my expense and carried on for more than twenty years.

But it had still been one of the best nights of my life. There was something special about the GIT, the camaraderie, the togetherness, the Knowing, the sense of mission. Out there in the woods, with two grand's worth of thermal imaging camera and your best mates who will do anything for you, who will do anything so we can change history together – I was going to miss that. I didn't know what I was going to do without it.

> • <

Beneath the murmur and small talk of the mourners, my highly evolved Knower's super-surveillance hearing skills detected a new sonic pattern: the *scratch-scratch* of heels on gravel. When I realised that the woman had paused behind me, I expected Maxine.

It was not Maxine. It was Boho, with her round face and soft, dimpled cheeks, vodka-bottle shoulders and wheaty blond hair tied up, her big, electric-blue eyes smiling at me like she's a nurse and I'd just come around from a savage beating.

'What are you doing here?' I said.

'Miss Cash says Uncle Gorgo, he die dressed as monkey, so I worry about you.'

'Where is Miss Cash?'

'Outside gate, with dangerous idiot.'

'She didn't give you a lift? Priceless.'

'I not ask for lift. I call Nigerian taxi.'

'You didn't need to come here. It's a funeral.'

'Uncle important to you, even though he make you sing like kipper.'

'Kippers are fish. They don't sing. They flop about. Now, Miss Cash, she's been singing like a canary. And Eddie, he stitched me up like a kipper. Get it?'

'Singing kipper is better.'

She slipped her hand into mine. I flinched when she squeezed it. The mourners outside the chapel parted and some of them shuffled towards us. The cortege had arrived. A man in a bowler hat led the hearse up the drive.

My chest started to tremble.

She tightened her squeeze on my hand.

She whispered something I didn't catch.

Story of my life.

> • <

When I first saw her photograph on meetukrainian-bridesnow.com, I knew that I was in love with her. Now, I think it was simply a matter of contrasts. For hours, I had been scanning blotchy, grainy images of sasquatches flitting through the backyards and forests of America, loping across highways and through rivers, swaying in cornfields, shatting-up campers – and then, bang, by fluke, beckoning to me from through the screen, a real, live human woman.

It was the image of her that I'd loved.

I suspect that she only liked the idea of me.

I fell in love with a jpeg.

I was hoaxed.

Meetukrainianbridesnow.com hoaxed me, too.

I can't blame Boho for that. The Internet hoaxed us both.

I'm not saying I don't appreciate how hard it was for her, coming to another, especially horrible country to escape poverty there, and having few options there besides slogging her guts out in a cement factory or doing fuck-all in a shitty mall worse than the ones we have here. Because she wanted more than that and some peace and some security and not some country where she feared there was going to be a war between animal-like men someday soon, she decided she would marry a man she didn't know for his not-very-much money when she didn't even speak the language. I wouldn't have had the conkers to do that. And if I'd wanted a quiet, obedient wife, I would have got a Thai bride like that Moppy from down the Churn, though that didn't work out for him as even she left him, or stabbed him, I can't remember which.

It must have been doubly difficult for Boho ending up with me, when you think about it. These marriage agencies, they can deceive both of you, and whatever her idea of me, I bet it wasn't master of skip logistics and hardcore

Knower. I'm not even sure that Sutton is a prettier place than Kharkov. I am sure that Boho is the prettiest woman from Kharkov in Sutton that I'll ever meet. There are just, as they say, 'language barriers' (aka I sometimes don't know what she is going on about), 'cultural differences' (aka 'there are no big monkeys in Sutton'), problems with 'priorities' (aka 'there *is* a dirty great gigantopithecus in Sutton, FACT'), and 'disagreements' about how to bring up children' (aka Kyrylo) and whether it should be held against you forever that you left him alone in a van while you chased the world's last great mystery across the Chipstead Downs Nature Reserve in the dead of night.

When we were first together, if she grew tired of the English exercises, we used to sit on the floor and make faces at each other. When amused, she wiggled her shoulders and her hair would shift from side to side. When something interested her, her eyes would widen to full beam and sometimes glisten. When she was cross, which was not that often to start with, she would close her eyes and mouth the numbers one to ten in Ukrainian. I taught her our numbers by playing bingo. Sometimes I wanted to know what she was really thinking, what her own language told her about the world that surrounded her now. She watched some right crap on the telly but I didn't mind. One of our first proper conversations was me telling her that she didn't have to cook for me three times a day every day, that it wasn't like that. I didn't need a skivvy. I had lived on my own for a long time. I could sling a pie in the oven every now and again. I remember an evening sat at a table outside a seafront pub in Cornwall and the light fading, the moon rising over the sea, and the darker the night grew and the drunker we became the more

beautiful she was to me. She told me about this man called
Mr Oliynyx who had too many dogs in iron cages, and who
kept promising to marry her when she knew this was not
what would happen. She told me about the holes in the road
that would never be filled unless she filled them herself.
She told me this heart-warming story about how under
the Communists her grandfather had run the biggest tyre
factory in north-eastern Ukraine. He had ruled with iron
fingers, apparently, and he'd never seen an Almasty, the
Russian Bigfoot, not even during the war. I remember that
I never took Boho to The Churn because the blokes in there
are fuckers. I took her to The Dog in Carshalton. It's more
sophisticated. And Kyrylo, I remember how tender and lit
up she was when he came along. I shouldn't have started it
up again then; the squatching, the GITing with Kyrylo. I
should have stayed a domestic Kev. I shouldn't have started
to dream about Bigfoot again, the Long Man, the Nonsuch
Kong, the North Surrey Gigantopithecus. I shouldn't have
started think that I could have everything, that I could solve
the great mystery and have my one chance of being a proper
dad and husband. But I am a Cell of One. I needed to Know.

> • <

Pallbearers carried the coffin into the chapel. We followed
the family inside. Organ music droned. The smell of the
flowers reminded me of the rich scent of the woods, the
whiff of freedom. We took a seat on the empty, right-hand
side of the chapel, which I assumed was reserved for the GIT
as the family had crammed themselves into the other side.
I was sure some of them were giving me the evils. Maybe

it was just my state of mind. We're all from Sutton, though. Maybe we can't help it.

I was about to ask Boho about Kyrylo, how he was and that, whether he would see me now, when Maxine and Derek Funnel sat down on the other side of her, both in dark suits, The Funnel's a flappy, long-tailed number. They both tried to look over at me. I didn't want to be looked at. Deep-blue curtains were still pulled across the cremator.

The coffin had been rested on the bier.

The music stopped.

A stocky minister with a bowl haircut appeared behind a lectern, a brass spread-eagle thing like something out of the Third Reich.

I had my head between my knees and I tried to shake it all out. The minister listed all the reasons why Edward Gartree was a great bloke, that he'd been a talented cameraman and worked on low-budget British horror films in the sixties and children's programmes in the seventies, and he'd loved his mum and The Crazy World of Arthur Brown and liked a round of golf and a pint in the pub and a laugh and a joke and a piss-take, and in the past he'd been involved in some ingenious April Fool's TV wheezes, where he'd filmed a rubber Tyrannosaurus rex in the grounds of a stately home near Dorking, and another where he conned little kids into believing spaghetti grew on trees abroad somewhere.

The minister didn't mention the GIT. Never once did he mention us. Never once did he mention me, who had been like a son to Eddie.

Throughout, my wife had her arm around my shoulders as I stared at the parquet tiles below, how they all fitted together so seamlessly. And it hit me there. I cried when

I didn't want to cry in front of anyone. He was gone. I'd never see him again. And he'd lied, he'd hoaxed me all this time, and even now I still wanted him back. I still wanted his advice and his friendship and passion for it. A cold feeling came for me, like someone had opened a door behind me and let in an icy blast. I'd felt it before, at Mum's funeral, when they put her in the ground, me and seven or eight sad and sorry Witnesses standing around the grave three days after I'd first seen the Gartree-Hogg footage; and that cold feeling happened to me, that feeling that he wasn't here, that I didn't know who either of us was, both of us were missing, but I needed him, I needed someone whether they were like Arthur C. Clarke or not. The next day I found Eddie's address in the phone book and wrote to him. I needed to do something, to be someone new now, to be there for someone else, or I'd stay at the grave forever. The icy blast at my back. The Red Darkness. The Kirtles. Those feelings were back. He was gone for good now, gone forever.

The curtains opened and the curtains closed behind the coffin.

> • <

We were all invited to Maxine's flat after the funeral. She'd ordered in wine and beer and prepared a buffet. Hexagon-shaped plates of miniature rabbit poo on crackers and orange chicken dippers that she called penang bites were placed on the surfaces of her breakfast bar.

Eddie never ate food like this. Nor did we. We ate scotch eggs and sausage rolls at Jackie Hogg's send-off. This wasn't a wake for Eddie. I knew this. The Funnel knew this. I expect even Bohuslava did, too.

This was a wake for the Gigantopithecus Intelligence Team.

No noise drifted in through the open balcony doors. Outside, it was Sutton. Sutton was dead. It probably always sounds dead on Thursday afternoons.

The Funnel had taken a glass of wine onto the balcony and gazed out at the distant trees. I hadn't had a chance to talk to him, find out how he was coping. I needed to talk to Maxine, too, but she was dealing with a kitchen spillage. I was stuck with Bohuslava.

'So, how's he doing?' I said.

'Once upon a time, Kevin, I invented a recipe for huntsman pie that I've forgotten.'

'Kyrylo? What's he up to?'

'Do you remember the pie, Kevin? How we made the pie?'

'I don't even know what's in a huntsman's pie.'

'On Wednesdays, Kyrylo goes team swimming. Maybe you could come over and help with pie?'

'He's in the swimming team?'

'Yes, and his grades are much better, and he's not smacked anyone in the mouth since Ms Cash has been mentoring him.'

I wanted desperately to hear all this, but somehow I couldn't stop fixating on the back of The Funnel's tumbleweed head and the dangling tails of his black frock coat. It is quite possible that nothing gigantopithical was going through The Funnel's mind. Oedipuss was around somewhere, and maybe The Funnel was simply trying to keep out of his way. He wouldn't want his groin slashed to doner meat again.

Maxine started to chime the side of a wine glass with a teaspoon. The Funnel shuffled in from outside. I'd never seen him shuffle before. He usually sprang. We assembled in front of Maxine. She refilled our glasses.

'I just want to say a few words about Edward,' she said. 'He was a character, and I'm sure that some of us are going to feel his loss keenly. And – Derek, Kevin – we were there, it was terrible. I'm sure it will take us a while to come to terms with what happened. And Kevin, whatever anyone said to you today—'

'Nobody said a word—'

'Don't take it to heart. None of us believe that you chased him into the road. Shhh. It wasn't your fault. We know it wasn't your fault. If it was anyone's fault, it was Edward's, and Mr Dawkers for driving without due care and attention. These matters have been dealt with, as we know. There's going to be a trial. We're going to have to go over all of this, so let's not go over it now.'

'He was a dirty great hoaxer.'

'And yes, he was a hoaxer. I've done a lot of digging, talked to a lot of people, today and previously, and it would seem Edward made a career out of public pranks—'

'Hoaxes.'

'Kevin, shush. This prank got out of hand, and badly out of hand for Edward, as really today, as he started all this, he should be here, with us, and we could all be sharing the joke, but it's not worked out like that. It all went too wrong for that. Eddie's wife has told me that for the last year, Eddie had been trying to raise funds for a comedy docudrama called *Believerz* in which a camera crew would follow some right idiots, i.e. us, who claim to have filmed an ape-man on

Banstead Common. Did you know that? No, of course you didn't. But listen, what we've had is an abject lesson in what happens when there's a failure of the method.'

Bohuslava tugged at the hem of my sleeve.

'We were too convinced,' said Maxine. 'We boxed ourselves in. We should have looked at what there was, and not even thought about something remarkable hiding among us. We should have stuck to the facts. If we'd done that, we'd never have been the victims of a hoax. And Edward would be here, having a laugh and a drink with us.'

The Funnel had his chin down. Strands of his hair hid his eyes.

'We should not waste any more time on this,' said Maxine. 'We should get back to our lives. Kevin, you're a very talented IT guy, and you're loyal and steadfast and have a lovely family. Derek, you're a...' I worried she was about to say 'devil-worshipping spawn of a fiend' or something, '... you're an amazing writer. We'd all like to see you make a success of that.'

The Funnel wasn't even listening. A frown stained his forehead. He was making a hundred calculations. He was weighing up the evidence. He was assessing the possibilities. He was asking questions. He was wrestling with the evidence of his own eyes. It stuck in my craw that it was The Funnel, not Eddie or me, who turned out to be the most hardcore of the Knowers.

He put his wine glass down on a glass coffee table with a hard click. He threw back his head. His hair flapped away from his eyes and he was clearly about to say his piece but Maxine swiped the air, the flat of her hand like a karate chop.

'Not now, Derek. Not again. This is over. We set out to prove something and it proved not to be true. It proved to be a hoax. There's only so long that a person can be hoaxed. Science will always be science.'

She raised her glass. Bohuslava and I raised our glasses, and reluctantly The Funnel did too.

'Edward,' said Maxine. 'Be at peace.'

'Gorgo,' I said. 'Cheers, mate.'

'Edward,' said The Funnel. 'All the old worship in this land is broken.'

'*Do pobachennya*,' said Bohuslava. 'Dippy tosspot.'

'I am going to get changed,' said Maxine. 'Please, imbibe.'

She disappeared into the hall, crossing paths with Oedipuss. The cat slunk into the room.

'*Ah kishka*,' said Bohuslava, stooping down to stroke his arched back.

When the cat hissed and The Funnel screamed I took advantage of the distraction to follow Maxine.

❯ • ❮

In the hallway, I ninja-styled myself onto the threshold. She'd already changed. With her back to me, she was buttoning up a pale blue cotton shirt. She must have already known what I was going to ask. We were joined now. We were beginning to act out each other's thoughts. We'd be finishing each other's sentences soon. There were still things we could share, teach each other when we headed back out there, went back to the woods.

On the slope, during those all-too-brief moments, when it was still possible, we had stood hand in hand, naked, fused, blessed by the great one, the Lord of the Trees, indestructible nature. We were a segment of his design. He had plans for us, he'd programmed our destiny, even if in the end he was just Eddie pissing about in the original, too-scary-for-kids Bungle Bear costume.

I needed to know if she'd experienced it too, if something had shifted in her life.

This is a longwinded way of saying that if I was ever going to tell her about how I really felt, I was going to have to do it now (aka before Boho could get me all confused).

I rapped my knuckles on the door.

'Jesus, Kevin. Usually it's polite to knock *before* you come in. Do you need the bathroom?'

'I was looking for you.'

'Let me finish getting changed. I'll come and join you.'

'Do you know what I don't understand?' I said. 'I mean, my head has been full of all sorts this last year, ever since you tiptoed into this thing of mine.'

'Kevin, you really are a sphinx inside a riddle sometimes.'

'Back then, when we were on the Common, were you inside my head? Did we share a moment?'

Her hands gently gripped the edge of the dresser. For the first time since we'd started to talk, she looked me in the eyes.

'Kevin, I think we did, yes.'

'Brilliant. It's not just me for once.'

'There was a moment, yes. Just for a second, for a split second, I was a Knower too. Just for a second I believed in it, I was like you.'

'Admit it: you loved it, all of it, going out with us, the kit, the woods, the waiting, the getting muddy. It's never going to be the same again.'

'It was just a shadow, it was nothing.'

'You're going to miss it, though, aren't you?'

'Chasing shadows?'

'Out in the woods, with the kit and the Knowers. You want that to end?'

'But there's nothing there. I concede there's a very remote chance that there might be relict hominids in the great spaces, but not in England, and certainly not in Sutton.'

'Come with me, then. Let's go to where they are. Let's go to the States, stick it up the Yanks. You and me. We'll find it. We're good at this. We'll win.'

'Kevin. All around the world, wherever these things are seen, it's just batty folklore, and a lot of people like Eddie trying to make easy money and make fools out of people like... us. Come on, you're better than that.'

'You just said it yourself, there's a remote chance.'

'There's a remote chance there's life on Mars.'

'Every disappointment is a step on the way to discovery, don't you see that?'

'Woolly thinking. Blind hope. Speculative punting. Haven't I taught you anything?'

Everything in my head felt like it was tumbling through my lungs and my guts, rolling me up with it as it plunged towards my feet.

'I love you,' I said. 'I want us to be together, out in the great space.'

She put her hands up before I'd even reached her.

'Don't be ridiculous, Kevin. Stop it. There's something else I need to tell you.'

'Yeah, Eddie. Turned out he was a dirty great hoaxer. And there's me, distracted by him for all this time. It's not here.

It's somewhere else. I shouldn't have restricted myself to the borough. You know, an English rectal hominid is called a woodwose, not a gigantopithecus. That was all an Eddie thing, a Sutton Cock thing. A woodwose is a little guy, about five feet. There's a load up in Lincolnshire, shatting-up dog walkers. The other day a carrot cruncher saw one scampering along a ditch near Spalding. We've got to get up there. Come with me.'

'Kevin, please sit down.'

'We'll do it properly Science this time. We won't make any assumptions until we've seen one.'

'There's something I need to tell you. Please, sit down.'

This time I did as I was told. I sat down on the bed. She towered above me, long and slim. She had this aloof expression on her face that was giving me a mild case of the Kirtles.

'Kevin, you're right... I have very much enjoyed being Lead Investigator of the GIT, despite everything. Despite the shouting, and Derek Funnel, and it all being a hoax – and it's all made me re-evaluate things.'

'You think it's real now?'

'I always knew it was a hoax. I just didn't know who the hoaxer was and how the hoax was achieved. Going out on expeditions, though, now that's made me realise how bored and unfulfilled I am by my job, which is basically crowd control, and I'm bored of Sutton and being here. You know, when I was little, it was all the stories of Victorian scientists going out into the world, adventuring from pole to pole, the voyage of the *Beagle*, Mary Anning and her plesiosaur – they made me want to be a scientist in the first place. I'd lost my way, and I'd lost my calling, all in the name of security and a regular salary. So I'd like to thank you, Kevin, for helping me find it again. I used to think you were just an immature idiot, a fantasist, a paranoid schizophrenic or something, a Lost Boy anyway, but you've got such a great capacity for wonder and I realise that I've needed to reconnect with my own.'

'You do want to come out with me again, don't you? You do want to take it to the States and stick it up the Yanks?'

'I've decided... I've accepted, Kevin, a role with a research team in Sumatra. I'm returning to my work with orangutans. I'm packing up tomorrow. I'll be off soon.'

'But, Max, we were together, on the Common—'

'That's what I'm saying, Kevin. Why don't you come with me?'

'With you?'

'Yes.'

'To Sumatra?'

'Yes.'

'To track the legendary orang pendek? Derek's already been over there and seen one.'

'Derek also thinks he's the reincarnation of Aleister Crowley. I went round for coffee. He's got a great gig shrine to To Mega Therion, the Great Beast, in his lounge.'

I shrugged. 'He's happy, though.'

'Kevin. Sumatra. On that night I first met you, in The Butterchurn, you said you'd relish an opportunity to explore a real jungle with real kit.'

'You want me to lead this crazy ride?'

'No. We need a porter.'

'A porter?'

'Yes, someone to look after the kit and carry it about. And you're also good with computers, data storage, cameras... I thought that might be up your strasse, and you'd get to see the jungle and the wildlife and the real magic of primates in their natural habitat. You'd learn how scientific research is conducted—'

'So we're not going looking for the orang pendek?'

'It's not our priority to look for it, but where we're going, Lake Gunung in the Kerinci Seblat National Park, it's unknown terrain, an unexplored interior, orangutans, tigers, yes, but the locals do have stories of the orang pendek and also the orang kardil, little men, not pongid but hominid, and giant pythons and the cigau, a big cat, like a homothere.'

'You want a porter, not a lead investigator?'

'Bit more than a porter, I suppose. Porter and IT support.'

'Not a secondary investigator?'

'Call it Master of Kit, if it makes you feel better.'

'I'm being passed over again.'

'It would be really good for you.'

'But I'm always more, like, the Lead Investigator.'

'You were never even Lead Investigator of the GIT. This would help put some distance between you and this, here, what happened, Eddie.'

'And you and me?'

'Kevin...' She shook her head.

'But, you and me, Max, we solved it. The mystery. The relict hominid...'

'Kevin, I used to think that if there is a relict hominid living among us in Sutton, it's you. It's *you*. You're the North Surrey Gigantopithecus. But now I realise that all those sightings and cases, they weren't simply made up, they were real. There was something in the woods, someone in the dark. It just wasn't what you wanted it to be, but it was there. Give Sumatra some thought. The orangutans are real, for now.'

She patted me on the shoulder as she drifted past me and out through the door.

› • ‹

I don't know how long I sat there, but it was long enough to realise that I was what she said I was before she said I could be her porter. A *very talented* IT guy. A Very Talented IT Guy who just wanted to make it up with his son now. The Very Talented IT Guy struggled up and dusted himself down. The Very Talented IT Guy ninja-styled into the breakfast bar area and grabbed a bottle of Belgian beer by the throat. Acoustic guitar music was playing. Over in the lounge, Maxine and Bohuslava swayed around each other. The Very Talented IT Guy tried not to have a weird fantasy involving a deserted campsite, three bottles of lemon vodka and Phil Collins's *Dance into the Light* CD on repeat. Out on the balcony, The Funnel had his back to the room, his wild tangle of hair haloed in sunlight. The Very Talented IT Guy sipped and watched the women dance. The Funnel seemed totally separate from their world. The Very Talented IT Guy now knew that their world is a great place to be. The Very Talented IT Guy just wanted to take his son somewhere and kick a ball about and buy a couple of Cornettos and a four-pack of non-Diet Coke and explain.

The Very Talented IT Guy could tell that Boho was already tipsy. Each time there was a lull in the music she would rise up on her tiptoes and slosh back one of Maxine's goblet-style wine glasses.

The Very Talented IT Guy sauntered over. Boho said something and wiggled her hips. Her hand appeared, palm up, and she wiggled her fingers at The Very Talented IT Guy.

Slipping his fingers in with hers would do The Very Talented IT Guy some good. The Very Talented IT Guy knew, though, that he couldn't give her any signal that things could go back to the way they were, not even for the sake of the boy. There could be no rebooting of the factory setting. The Very Talented IT Guy knew that even if there were to be no others, ever, he could not have said all those things to Maxine in the bedroom and then leave this flat with his former wife as if nothing had happened. The Very Talented IT Guy realised that he was only able to compute this as he was no longer a Lost Boy, only a Lonely Man.

Boho was now cupping her hand as if she were waiting for something to be dropped into her palm.

> • <

Out on the balcony, alongside the Funnel, the full force of the light cracked some shell that cased my skin. Suddenly, I was myself again. Totally myself.

The Funnel didn't acknowledge me at first. He was standing, head back, chin out, hands locked behind his back as if he was strapped to the mast of a storm-tossed galleon.

'All right, spanner,' I said. 'How's it been?'

'Interesting.'

'Well, yeah, you can say that.'

'Interesting, and solitary.'

'Oh c'mon, geez. We were close, me and Eddie. I had stuff to think through.'

'So did I.'

'Like who you are this week? Talking of which, Sci-Borg Max just told me that you're not just a fanboy, you think you're actually whatisface Crowley—'

'Do you think Crowley achieved what he achieved by merely thinking?'

'You're going to have to fill me in on that one day, hopefully over half a dozen of these cold little friends.'

I swigged my beer so he wouldn't see I was laughing. I'd not had a laugh for a long time, I realised.

'Seriously, you doing okay?' I said. 'This has been the stresstaurant at the end of the universe.'

'I slept with faith and found a corpse in my arms on awakening.'

'You never told me you were deep like that, Del.'

'Crowley said that.'

'Been catching up on your reading, then. Probably a wise move.'

'Not Crowley. I have been undertaking my own research. Has she given you the so-called "official version"?'

'There's no unofficial version. We saw him: Eddie, in a suit, dead on the road. We've got to admit we've been hoaxed to buggery this time. I can't get my head around it any other way.'

'It's part of the grander plan, Kevin. Edward sacrificed himself to save the Long Men from premature exposure. Edward led us to the amulet and then set himself ablaze as a distraction. You must not listen to those who don't cut their own way through the jungle.'

'Funny you should say that, because Maxine just invited me to go with her to the jungle. As her butler, obviously—'

'Will you go?'

'Eddie was like a father to me, but now I've got to be a father to someone else.'

'You've always asserted that you're not kitted out for civilian life.'

'No, I've always said that I wanted to prove to my boy that it lived among us so I could be with him. Now, I've just got to hope he's able to blank out most of his childhood. They can do that, kids.'

'You're talking to me here, Kevin, not your social worker.' He relaxed his rigid pose, turned to face me fully. 'Don't tell me, Kevin, that since the ambush you haven't thought about a solo career? Don't tell me that afterwards you thought that I, Tom Egatherion, would crumble and you would be left to carry on alone.'

'Okay, I admit it, I did.'

'So did I. I knew you would crumble first.'

'Bollocks. What were you going to call the group then?'

'Alien Primate Expedition. APE.'

'Well, I was going to call mine Sutton Hominid Investigation Team.'

'An excellent moniker.'

'We can join forces now. We can be APESHIT. Satisfied?'

'We've got ourselves into trouble with acronyms before.'

'Yeah, and who gave us that acronym? Eddie. We got ourselves into trouble because of hoaxing.'

'The hoax is not the hoax, Kevin. Think about it. This whole explanation of Maxine's, it's too convenient, it's too unlikely and complicated. There is another, more logical explanation of what went on that night, what happened to Edward. We need to honour his sacrifice and return to the fray. This was not the end. We are closer now than ever before. They don't want you to realise that.'

'I don't want to hear this. Have another glass of wine.

Smoke some crack or something. This music might sound better then.'

I glanced back over my shoulder at Maxine and Boho. The music had changed. They had used Maxine's crap laptop to pipe some Ukrainian folk music off the Internet. Boho was showing Maxine how to do this dance routine they do in barns over there that any minute now was going to get psychotically fast. Boho had tried to get me to learn these moves once but I broke a lava lamp, Kyrylo's radio-controlled racing car, and one of her toes. They were celebrating. I didn't particularly like the idea that they were celebrating, but I had half a mind to rejoin them.

I felt bad for The Funnel, though. I didn't want to leave him on his own.

Over in the distance, the Surrey Hills looked to me like the grey-blue humps of a Loch Ness Monster. A misty haze outlined the slopes. The last remaining clumps of Andreasweald poked out, once thick and impassable but now broken up by settlements and suburbs, roads and railways.

I stared out at this place and tried to think of it as something understandable: an ecosystem, an economy, home, a place to be. Then the Very Talented IT Guy told me that a forest is just a pre-technology information network, software for the soil's hardware. The Very Talented IT Guy allowed Sutton itself to be his focus and tried not to wonder what the man beside him watched out over, if all he saw, too, were grey office blocks where people punched information into machines and answered phone calls and spoke in boring voices and made presentations that would lead to money moving from one company to another, and tried to ignore the vast, unsettled energy fields that crackled inside them as they drove back and forth between work and home twice a day. The Very Talented IT Guy wondered if the real day was only the day you met your wife, or your wife met you, or when new people were born and your uselessness was fended off for sixteen or so years, when none of it, for an instant, could be reduced to a point on a graph or a stage in a five-year plan.

Down below, in the street beyond the garden that surrounded this particular apartment building, a silvery car pulled up in the middle of the road, obstructing the traffic behind it. A man got out, flustered, red-faced. A horn sounded, then another. The red-faced man hammered on the door of a house. Another shell of a man emerged. They shouted at each other. Horns blared. The shell of a man put his hands up, marched past the red-faced man, and moved his own car from where it was parked outside the house next door. The red-faced man waved at the obstructed cars behind his own, and then just about pulled off a parallel parking manoeuvre. The shell of a man stomped back into his house, muttering, his fists twitching at his sides. The other cars now passed through. The first of the drivers flicked the Vs at the red-faced man. The Very Talented IT Guy tried to accept that he too was like those people down there: the red-faced man, the shell of a man, and the jeering drivers for whom this had been the only moment today when their hearts had truly worked the blood through their veins. After this, the day would fizzle out into another called tomorrow.

Behind us, the music in the room sped up and pitched.

'This is it,' said The Funnel. 'All you want to know is here.'

Something shimmered in the palm of his hand.

Glinting, goldish.

DJ Brunt's pendant.

Or, as it became known to us, The Amulet of Machapuchare, Key to the Last Gate.

FACT.

Shangri La Village Resort
Pokhara
Nepal

30 August ███

Dear Kyrylo,

It's been on my mind since I got here that
we didn't see each other before I left.
It wasn't that I didn't want to see you.
I was, to be frank, desperate to see you,
but your mum said you still weren't ready
to talk to me even when she'd told you I
wasn't doing it any more. That turns out
to be more complicated than she thought
at the time, but I am very hopeful that
writing it all down now will prove things
to you about me and about us. I hope
that when I get back, you will realise
what it's all about and we can finally
have that catch-up and kick-about I have
wanted to have with you for so long.
  I did - you must believe me - have to
get away sharpish before things overtook
me. Sometimes you get a gut instinct,
you'll see, but sometimes you know people
are going to cage you in and stop you
following your dreams. I am going to

come back, but in case it's a long time, son, I want you to always trust your gut instinct and follow your dreams, whatever they are, even if other people poke fun at you. It's not easy being a Stubbs, but it's the Stubbs way.

I know that things have not been easy and I have not made things easy for you, when that was all I ever wanted. I would also like to say here, categorically, that I am truly sorry for that time I left you in the van. You've got to believe me, I was on a mission. My priorities became confused.

But even saying all that, I do want you to know the facts and I want you to know them from me, so you know they're definitely the truth. Somewhere is a dossier that one day will give you my side and my take on the first part of the Giganto story. That's one of the things I've been doing since I got here. Writing it all up, so there's a record. I've given it to someone who will one day give it to you.

I did think I was done with all of it after Uncle Eddie's death, but when Uncle Derek showed me that mystical artefact when we were on Ms Cash's balcony, I knew that there was another, more convincing explanation for what had happened, that Eddie hadn't hoaxed us and the gigantopithecus was still out there, waiting for us all shimmery and holy grail. That's why I decided to come to Nepal with Uncle Derek and give Giganto one last best shot.

This is much better than going to a desert island with Ms Cash and poking an adder, or working in an office, if I'm honest (though there's nothing wrong with that if that is what you end up wanting to do with your life, I will back you to the hilt whatever).

We've been here about ten days. The town's a bit funky and the people are all right. Bit smiley, though, when they're not trying to flog you a tent or kill you. The death threats happened further in, nearer to where we're going, closer to the place they call The Sanctuary. That day trip was all part of the build-up, reconnaissance, sussing out the lay of the land, all the stuff I've been training for all my life. We've been planning during the day and getting our heads straight during the evenings, when it's cooler and you can think. Uncle Derek goes off to commune with this special amulet we've discovered and get into an otherworldly place. He's got to come up trumps on this score. While he does that, I've been writing it all up. It's for you, the writing, that's how I think of it, but it's also for the world, a sort of prologue to the story to come, the story of the Great Expedition that started in Sutton and continues here.

So, this is it. Tomorrow, we, Uncle Derek and your old man, are going to scale Machapuchare.

The thing is - and this is where you're going to be really proud of me - no one has ever climbed this mountain before. No one has ever got to the top of Machapuchare before Uncle Derek and your old man. In 1957, some posh knobs nearly got there but they bottled it. Since then, the locals have banned climbing it. This is where it gets interesting. They reckon the god Shiva the Destroyer lives up there. When snow gusts off in great clouds from the peak, that's Shiva burning mystic incense. The mountain is supposed to be sacred. You can't go up there. They get the right hump if you do.

That's the thing about religion. It's just one group of people insisting that they're right when they're wrong. If you'd ever met your gran, you'd understand this better.

It's gigantic, 23,000 feet up in the air, you've got to bribe a Sherpa to get a cab out there, and last Thursday we got close to the foot of the mountain until all these people came out of these shacks and fired a rifle three times; but we are going back, though. We are going up tomorrow, two nutters from Sutton. We know that on top of that mountain is The Gate, and it's through The Gate that they get in. That's what The Clown says. The Clown is the Key.

We don't call it The Clown now. We call it by its proper name, the name Uncle Derek looked up in one of his books. We call it The Key to the Last Gate.

Tomorrow we will take The Key to The Last Gate to the Last Gate. Through The Last Gate is their world. We will see everything. We will meet them there. We will come back with everything that there is to Know. We will come back heroes. FACT.

I want you to know that I'm doing this for you, son. It's always been for you. I will come back with proof. We can be mates again. I love you, son, and writing things out like this is the hardest bit of all for me. I want you to know that I will return soon and that you must not worry. I am lit up with excitement here. Proper lit up. I have been waiting for this moment for all my life. Tomorrow, we head for the mountain.

Love from

Dad

ACKNOWLEDGEMENTS

Gigantic could not have been possible without the inspiration provided by: 2000AD, 2001: A Space Odyssey, Arthur C Clark's Mysterious World, Buck Rogers in the Twenty-Fifth Century, Bungle from Rainbow, Chewbacca, Phil Collins, Conan the Barbarian, Aleister Crowley, Doctor Who and the Web of Fear, Judge Dredd, James Herbert, King Kong, CS Lewis, the Geoff Love Orchestra, HP Lovecraft, David Lynch, Marillion, Gustav Meyrink, Omni, the Patterson-Gimlin Film, the Piltdown Man, Abe Sapien, Tarzan, Lord of the Jungle and The Unexplained.

Thank you, too, and much respect to:

Dan Coxon, Nicolas Ruston, George Sandison and Jonathan Taylor

The Secret Order of the Golden Lockdown: Glenn Ogden, Kersten Hall, Chris Otter, Jonathan McMaster and Andy Downes

Staff and students at the Unthank School

Catsaus

ABOUT THE AUTHOR

Ashley Stokes was born in Carshalton, Surrey in 1970 and educated at St Anne's College, Oxford and the University of East Anglia. He is the author of *Touching the Starfish* (Unthank Books, 2010) and *The Syllabus of Errors* (Unthank Books, 2013), and edited the *Unthology* series and *The End: Fifteen Endings to Fifteen Paintings* (Unthank Books, 2016). His short fiction has appeared in, among others: *Black Static*, *Tales from the Shadow Booth*, *BFS Horizons* and *Out of Darkness* (edited by Dan Coxon). He lives in Norwich.